Kate entered the ~~room~~, ~~and then~~ stopped dead. Standing with his back to the window was the blond giant who had nearly run into her that afternoon.

He grinned at her surprise. 'So, we meet again, Sister; how very fortuitous.'

'What do you mean,' Jonathan asked truculently, 'you've met before?'

While she was fumbling for words, Rowland North said in an amused tone, 'Nothing formal, Jonathan— you might say that we almost bumped into each other.'

Kate spoke at last.

'Actually, Jonathan, Dr North almost bumped into me when I stopped to avoid running over a dog. His reflexes were almost as good as mine.'

Rory gave a great shout of laughter. '*Touché*,' he said.

Jonathan looked relieved, though he obviously didn't understand the barbed remark that Kate had made.

Kate realised then that her hand was still engulfed in Rory's. She made to withdraw it, but found that she was unable to do so. He squeezed it gently and said, 'How do you do?' and, in a polite, social voice, 'It really is a pleasure to meet you.' He smiled, and to her surprise this time the smile reached his eyes.

Margaret O'Neill was born in Portsmouth in 1926. She started scribbling at the age of four and began nursing at twenty. She contracted TB, and when recovered, she did her British Tuberculosis Association nursing training before going on to general training at the Royal Portsmouth Hospital, near the dockyard.

She married another student, a Latvian, and had two children, a son who is now a designer, and a daughter who is an actress and drama teacher. With her late husband she owned and managed several nursing homes, and though now retired, she still has many nursing and medical contacts. Her husband encouraged her writing and would have been delighted to see her books in print. Margaret now lives in Sussex, and loves gardening, reading and writing.

Previous Title

COTTAGE HOSPITAL

A QUESTION OF HONOUR

BY

MARGARET O'NEILL

MILLS & BOON LIMITED
ETON HOUSE   18–24 PARADISE ROAD
RICHMOND   SURREY   TW9 1SR

First published in Great Britain 1991
by Mills & Boon Limited

© Margaret O'Neill 1991

Australian copyright 1991
Philippine copyright 1991
This edition 1991

ISBN 0 263 77499 6

Set in 10 on 11 pt Linotron Times
03-9112-57115
Typeset in Great Britain by Centracet, Cambridge
Made and printed in Great Britain

CHAPTER ONE

IF ONLY it would rain, thought Kate as she peered through the car window at the blanket of heavy grey cloud above. The heat, on this late September afternoon, was oppressive; it had been building up for days. Every tree and garden was coated with an end-of-season dust. The road and pavement of the High Street, looking as uniformly grey as the skies, wound down the hill between the ancient buildings like an unwashed ribbon.

She would be glad to get back to the health centre and make up her report, although, because of old Dr North's heart attack, there would be a whole load of extra problems for her to deal with. She wasn't likely to get off duty till seven or even later.

There was a flash of lightning over the distant hills visible across the valley, where the High Street petered out into the square beside the river. A rumble of thunder swept over the small market town. It was nothing alarming coming from a long way off. The second rumble was closer, preceded by a brilliant flash of light, and the third, a great crack overhead, was almost simultaneous with a fork of lightning zigzagging above the roof of the town hall bell-tower.

Kate braked as hard as she could when a small dog appeared in front of her. It squealed with fright and dived on to the pavement. At that moment, the heavens opened and great penny pieces of rain began to beat down. Within seconds these had fused together in one continuous sheet, and the steep street was suddenly filled with rushing water.

The dog had disappeared. As fast as she was able,

Kate started winding up the windows. Already the rain was pelting in on the seats.

A voice, raised above the din of thunder and rain beating on the roof of the car, shouted in her ear.

'What the hell are you thinking of, stopping like that? You nearly caused an accident. I only just braked in time.'

A strong brown hand held down the driver's window that she was trying to close. A lean face topped with wet bronze-blond hair bent to stare at her with cool sea-green eyes through the half-shut window.

Kate shouted back. 'A dog—a dog ran in front of me; I had to stop. Sorry.'

'A dog?' queried the man, still holding down her window. 'What dog?' He sounded as if he didn't believe her.

Kate shrugged. 'I don't know, it's gone.' And belatedly, 'I hope it's all right; it was very frightened.'

She became aware of the pelting rain and—in spite of a raincoat draped round his shoulders—the drenched figure of the man who was interrogating her. The traffic on the other side of the road had sorted itself out and was starting off again. She wondered about the pile-up of vehicles that might be behind her.

'We'd better move on,' she said. 'The traffic builds up quickly here.'

'And what about this poor creature that you nearly ran down? Are we going to leave it to make another death-defying dash across the line of traffic?'

Kate had been wondering about this herself. There was no sign of the dog, or its owner. In fact, Kate was pretty sure that it was Miss Thomson's dog—a small Yorkshire terrier. If it was, the devoted mistress would not be far away. In fact it surprised her that she was not around.

At that moment, Miss Thomson materialised beside the blond giant, who still kept a restraining hand on

Kate's car window. In her arms Miss Thomson was holding Mufty.

'Oh, Sister Christy, I am sorry; I do apologise for Mufty's behaviour, but it wasn't really his fault. He slipped his collar and the thunder frightened him.'

Well, that's one in the eye for you, mate! thought Kate, giving the stranger a disarmingly sweet smile. More or less accusing me of dreaming up a dog!

'It's all right, Miss Thomson, no harm done,' she said to reassure that lady. 'Perhaps you should tighten Mufty's collar, and you'd better get indoors or you'll both drown.'

The interrogator had laid a comforting hand on the small dog's head while this conversation was going on, and now made conciliatory noises to Miss Thomson.

'Have you far to go?' he asked. 'I should be happy to give you a lift.'

He cast a malicious smile in Kate's direction, clearly indicating that she might have thought to make this offer.

Before Miss Thomson, who was clearly pleased with the attention she was receiving, could reply, Kate said kindly but with a victorious edge in her voice, 'Miss Thomson lives there——' she pointed across the passenger seat '—in the flat above the tearooms.'

'Then allow me to escort you to the door, dear lady,' said the stranger, offering an arm and giving Kate a frosty smile. Solicitously, and, Kate thought, with overdone charm, he guided Miss Thomson round Kate's car and up the brick garden path to the front door.

Kate made a face at his retreating back and started off down the hill. There were several cars queueing behind the beastly man's Lotus, unable to pass in the face of oncoming traffic.

'Good,' she said to herself. 'Let him sort it out, since he seems to think he's so damned clever.'

The rain was a blessing. The thunder had stopped,

and it was really quite pleasant driving through the steady downpour after weeks of drought. Kate felt pleased with herself. Her tiny triumph over the bossy stranger had lifted her spirits. Even the knowledge that she would have a pile of work to attend to before going off duty couldn't deflate her.

Mary Potts, the elderly receptionist who had worked for old Dr North since the world began, was on duty.

'There are several patients booked to see you,' she hissed, as Kate, very wet from her short dash from the car, entered the reception area. 'And Dr Jonathan wants to see you before you start on them.' She looked infuriatingly smug. 'He's in a towering rage about something, so even you had better watch yourself.'

She was the only senior member of staff who addressed Dr North's son as Dr Jonathan. Everyone else called him Jonathan or young Dr North. It was as if by clinging to some antiquated form of address Miss Potts underlined her status as the longest-serving member of staff. She was also the only member of Midchester's medical centre who disapproved of Kate and Jonathan's close friendship. A friendship which had for a long time teetered on the edge of something more serious, more lasting.

'He could do so much better for himself,' she was quoted as saying. 'The Norths are an old county family. He could marry anyone he chooses.'

The general opinion among several of Kate's colleagues was the opposite. Many thought that she was too good for him. It wasn't that he was actively disliked, for he could be charming and he was a moderately good doctor, but it was obvious to the more observant that he was a weak sort of character. Friends worried that he would constantly lean on her, and they felt that she had enough to cope with, without another dependant.

'Oh, well, I'd better beard the lion in his den, hadn't

I?' Kate apologised to the patients who were waiting for her. 'The storm held me up,' she explained. 'I'll only be a few minutes now.'

There was a concerted, 'That's all right, Sister,' as she made for Jonathan's door, removing the raincoat that she'd slung around her shoulders as she went.

She knocked and entered. He was sitting at his desk, handsome head bowed in his hands, looking not angry, as Potty had suggested, but defeated.

'Jonathan, what's the matter?' she asked, moving quickly to his side and putting an arm round his shoulder.

'Look, read that.' He thrust a single sheet of thick notepaper into her hand. 'I can't believe that Dad would do this. I think that bloody cousin of mine is inviting himself; it's just the sort of thing he would do, to get back into Dad's good books.'

Kate looked at the bold, neat writing and read in silence.

Dear Jonathan,

Uncle Matt appears to have heard that I am waiting to take up another appointment. He has asked me to help out in the practice pro tem while you are short-handed, and I am happy to do this if it will assist in his recovery.

I'm sure that we can put aside past differences while I am at Midchester, for the good of the practice and your father's peace of mind.

Expect me soon. I will telephone with a firm time of arrival.

Yours,
Rory.

'He sounds a bit pompous,' said Kate, 'but hardly a threat. Look, I know what you've told me about him, but it's said that blood's thicker than water. He must feel that. You need help with the work; what could be more natural than that your father should ask him to come and give a hand? From what I've heard, Dr North did enough for him in the past. Your cousin probably sees this as a chance to repay him for that.'

'What—after the way he behaved, walking out on Dad but letting him support him through med school? You must be joking; he's out for what he can get—like a share, if not all, of the practice.'

Kate had her doubts about this. Based on what she had heard over the years, it seemed that, contrary to general belief at the time, Rowland North was not entirely to blame for his sudden departure.

Mrs North, Matthew's pretty but feckless wife, had been very vocal about Rory's lack of appreciation for what his uncle had done for him. She had certainly fuelled the rumours about his going, and hinted at something even more unsavoury than an almighty row being the reason.

Nobody seemed to know the truth, except Matthew North and his nephew, and the one wasn't prepared to comment, and the other had left Midchester for good. But people who had known Rory well had, over the years, expressed their doubts about the reasons for his leaving his uncle's home in apparent disgrace. It just didn't tally with the young man's character.

Jonathan, who had been away at school, had chosen to believe the worst and continued to do so. But Kate thought that this was more in defence of his mother's version of the event than a true appraisal of the situation. Though she'd heard that he'd been devastated at the time, since his much older cousin had been something of a hero in his eyes.

She knew from experience that it would be useless to put all this to him now; he was not in a mood to listen to sweet, or any other, reason.

'Look, we'll talk about it later. I must go and see to some patients and your evening surgery will be starting soon.' Kate bent and kissed him lightly on the cheek. 'Perhaps he'll be too busy to come after all.'

'He's on his way,' said Jonathan in a hopeless sort of voice. 'He phoned earlier this afternoon.' Hopelessness turned to a bitter sneering tone. 'You can bet your bottom dollar he's not going to lose the opportunity to take over here.'

Kate felt helpless against his determined resentment and self-pity.

'Look, I have to go; we'll sort it out later.' She fled to her small surgery and buzzed for her first patient.

All the time she was syringing Mrs Jackson's ears and carrying on a conversation with the patient, she thought of Jonathan and his paranoiac resentment of his cousin Rory.

It was a stalemate situation that was almost impossible to deal with. How could one reconcile two men so diametrically opposed to each other? No, she amended, it didn't sound, from the tone of his letter, as if Rory was hostile to Jonathan to any degree.

'There, Mrs Jackson; they should be clear now for quite a while,' she assured the lady, a regular for syringing. 'I'll just swab the surplus solution out.' Delicately she used a wisp of cotton wool, wound round an orange stick, to mop up the moisture. She removed the little plastic cape from the patient's shoulders. 'All done.'

Mrs Jackson stepped down from the surgical chair and gave Kate a warm smile. 'It is nice coming to see you, Sister,' she said. 'You always make me feel better, as well as making me hear better.'

'Well, thank you,' said Kate, rather surprised by the compliment. She opened the door. 'Ask the next patient to come in, please, Mrs Jackson.'

'Will do.'

Mr Lakey came in. 'You said that you'd take these

stitches out today, Sister,' he said before he was halfway into the room. 'If you think they're ready.'

'Let's have a look.' Kate removed the dressing covering the wound across the palm of his hand. 'That's fine, Mr Lakey,' she said after examining the long diagonal cut. 'All healed up; the stitches are certainly ready to come out.'

She swabbed the area with antiseptic and, with a few deft snips of the stitch-scissors and gentle easing with forceps, removed the skin sutures.

Mr Lakey was followed by Mrs Napier, who needed an anti-tetanus booster, and was quickly dealt with.

Unless Jonathan or Dr Lyons—Rachel—wanted anything done for a patient, Kate was finished in the surgery for the evening. She tidied up, went through to her office and prepared to attack the mound of paper-work that awaited her.

It was about a quarter of an hour later that Mary Potts knocked at her door and almost fell into the room before Kate had time to answer.

'You'll never guess who's come,' she said in an excited, shrill voice, 'not in a million years!'

Kate knew immediately who it must be.

'Dr Rowland North,' she said, teasing Potty by trying to sound rather bored, though in reality she was as excited as the receptionist at the prospect of meeting the infamous Rory.

Potty gasped. 'How did you know—he's only just arrived?' She remembered Kate's interview with Jonathan earlier. 'Of course, Dr Jonathan told you. That's why he was so cross; he'd heard that his cousin was coming. There's no love lost between them you know, which isn't surprising when you think——'

She was interrupted by the desk-bell ringing loudly and a patient facetiously shouting, 'Shop!' just as Kate's internal phone buzzed.

It was Jonathan on the phone.

'Sister, will you come to my room, please?' he said formally in a sombre voice. 'There's someone I must introduce to you.'

It would, she thought, have been more natural to say that he wanted her to meet someone, but, presuming that it was his cousin, that wouldn't be true.

'Come,' he said sharply as she knocked at his door.

Kate entered, and then stopped dead. Standing with his back to the window was the blond giant who had nearly run into her that afternoon.

He grinned at her surprise. 'So, we meet again, Sister; how very fortuitous.' He stepped forward and held out the strong brown hand that had so recently prevented her from winding up the car window.

Kate felt her hand, which she had automatically put forward, enclosed in his large one. Jonathan stared at them both.

'What do you mean,' he asked truculently, 'you've met before?' He turned a questioning face towards Kate. 'Kate?'

For the life of her she couldn't find her tongue. While she was fumbling for words, Rowland North said in an amused tone, 'Nothing formal, Jonathan—you might say that we almost bumped into each other.' He grinned widely, revealing large white even teeth, but the smile didn't reach his eyes, Kate noticed. They remained the same as before: cool, sea-green, impersonal.

Kate spoke at last.

'Actually, Jonathan, Dr North almost bumped into me when I stopped to avoid running over a dog. His reflexes were almost as good as mine.'

Rory gave a great shout of laughter. '*Touché*,' he said.

Jonathan looked relieved, though he obviously didn't understand the barbed remark that Kate had made. 'So you haven't met properly before, then?' Kate shook her head. 'But you know that this is my cousin, Rory North, Rory, this is Sister Christy, our manager.' He made no attempt to reveal her Christian name.

Kate realised then that her hand was still engulfed in Rory's. She made to withdraw it, but found she was unable to do so. He squeezed it gently and said, 'How do you do?' and in a polite, social voice, 'It really is a pleasure to meet you.' He smiled, and to her surprise this time the smile reached his eyes. They remained as green as ever, but the remote, cool look had gone, and she saw that they were speckled with golden flecks of light.

'How do you do?' she replied as politely as he had done. He released her hand. Kate turned to Jonathan. 'I must go and get on,' she said in an impersonal, professional voice, 'unless you want me for anything else.'

'Yes, of course. Shall I see you later?' He sounded pathetically unsure of himself.

'Certainly; we're going out for a drink, aren't we, unless your cousin's arrival makes that impossible?' She was determined that the self-assured Rory shouldn't walk all over Jonathan, who seemed already thrown by his presence.

'Oh, please don't let me interfere with your plans,' he interjected before Jonathan could open his mouth. 'I'm having supper with Uncle Matt. We've a lot to catch up on.'

He stepped in front of Kate and opened the door for her.

'See you again, Sister; I'll be grateful for your help tomorrow when I start work.'

Kate marched out, well aware that he had taken command, and more or less dismissed her. Angrily, she wondered why Jonathan hadn't been more forthright. After all, it was his room, and he was the senior doctor in the partnership now that his father was ill.

She returned to her office and the ever-present mountain of paperwork still sitting on her desk.

'Well, he's not going to ride roughshod over me,' she vowed out loud, as she tackled the next week's duty roster.

CHAPTER TWO

KATE settled herself on the oak bench while Jonathan went to fetch the drinks. He came back with her dry Martini and his half of real ale, and the bar menu.

'I thought we should have something to eat,' he said. 'I'm starving. What about a ploughman's?'

'Great, I only had a scratch meal when I got home.'

He went to the bar and ordered their food. When he came back he asked, 'Problems?' referring to her remark about a hurried meal.

Although he seemed mildly interested, Kate had the feeling, as she so often did with Jonathan, that it was only a polite enquiry. He asked for her sake, and not out of concern for her invalid mother or her small nephew.

She shrugged. 'Nothing that couldn't be dealt with.'

She might have enlarged upon the situation that had greeted her when she'd arrived home, but he ran a hand through his dark curly hair and then stroked his neat beard. It was a familiar and unconscious gesture. To Kate it was a signal to change the subject.

She sipped her drink and asked, 'How did things go with your father and your cousin this evening? Do you think that they will be able to put the past behind them?'

'Oh, they're getting on like a house on fire. Bosom pals. You'd never know that Rory practically killed Dad when he walked out twenty years ago.'

Trying to sound both sympathetic and sensible, Kate suggested, 'Perhaps your father had second thoughts about why Rory left. Maybe he feels that he wasn't entirely to blame for what happened.'

Jonathan stared at her in disbelief.

'What the hell are you saying?' he ground out angrily. 'That my mother made it all up? That dear Cousin Rory didn't try to pinch some of her jewellery to pay off some gambling debt?'

Kate was amazed. She'd never heard anything about jewellery or debts—only that Rowland North had left Midchester under a cloud and had caused his uncle great distress. Now, even if rumour had suggested it, having met the man concerned, she wouldn't have believed such a thing. Of course, the mature man might be a totally different person from the eighteen-year-old of twenty years ago, but dishonest, now or in the past? Never. She couldn't, wouldn't believe it. Even her brief acquaintance with Dr Rowland North made the idea unthinkable.

Yet Jonathan seemed so certain, *too* certain, perhaps. . .protesting too much? He'd never mentioned anything about stealing before, though he'd often spoken of his cousin. It seemed to be a subject that he couldn't leave alone. Kate had concluded that it was because he had rather hero-worshipped his cousin when he was a boy, and felt let down by him when he left. If there was any truth in what he had just said, surely there would have been at least a hint about it in the garbled tales that had circulated over the years?

Jonathan said in a low, passionate voice, 'Don't you believe me? Do you think that I would make up something like that?'

'No, of course not, but you've never mentioned it before. I thought that nobody really knew why Rory went so suddenly, except your father, and of course your mother.'

'Are you suggesting that Mother deliberately framed him?' He sounded rather like a small boy accused of cheating, she thought, and was ashamed of her disloyalty.

For a fleeting moment, Kate wondered just that. Mrs North had died only last year, and Jonathan still grieved for her. She had, in all the years that Kate had known her, been a rather strange lady. Surely it wasn't beyond the bounds of possibility that she had embroidered the truth for her own peculiar reasons? Jonathan might or might not be aware of this, but he would certainly protect her memory if he felt called upon to do so. Perhaps Mrs North was at the bottom of the mystery surrounding Rory's actions all those years ago, and old Dr North knew it.

Possibly Jonathan knew it too, but wouldn't admit it even to himself. He looked very vulnerable. The arrival of his cousin had upset him more than she had at first realised.

She said softly, 'I don't want to argue with you, Jonathan. We've both had a busy day. Please let's drop the subject for the moment.' She touched his hand gently. 'Darling, forget your beastly cousin, just for now, anyway. Everything will seem much better in the morning.'

Jonathan's anger evaporated. He gave her a pleading look. 'As long as you stick by me,' he said, 'I'm not going to let him take over you as well as everything else.'

'He's not going to take over anything. You're the boss—just let him know that. And don't worry about me. I think that he's the most arrogant and conceited bloke that I've met in a long time.'

'Do you really?' Jonathan looked pleased and relieved.

'Really,' she said with all the conviction she could muster. 'Come on, let's eat, for heaven's sake; I've got a great gap where some food should be.'

He laughed at that. 'You're wonderful,' he said, squeezing her hand and leaning across the table to brush her cheek with his lips. 'Such a sense of humour.'

At that moment somebody brought their food from the bar kitchen.

Kate grinned and her cheeks dimpled. 'Which needs feeding as much as the rest of me,' she said with a laugh, before sinking her teeth into a crusty roll.

She was quite unconscious of how lovely she looked in the soft light of the wall-lamps. Her long straight hair, a dark, gleaming chestnut, streamed down her back, released from the neat chignon that she wore when on duty. Her warm brown eyes sparkled with the happiness she felt at having Jonathan out of his despair. The soft tan that she had acquired over the long, hot summer was enhanced now by the lamplight, and her slightly olive skin glowed with health.

Jonathan stopped eating and stared at her. To him at that moment she had never seemed more beautiful or desirable. What am I waiting for? he asked himself. He leaned across the table and laid a detaining hand on hers as she was about to take another bite at her roll. 'Kate,' he said huskily, 'will you——?'

A great blast of noise drowned his words. Kate saw his lips moving soundlessly. There was a tremendous roaring in her ears. Everything shook. She was picked up by some unseen force, and thrown to the floor. She heard herself shriek as lumps of plaster and then a huge oak beam fell, missing her by inches. Choking dust swirled everywhere. She couldn't see Jonathan through the thickening mass that rained down from above. She called to him, but there was no answer. She heard cries and other voices calling from what seemed a long way off.

White plaster particles covered her. Carefully she picked a few pieces from her hair. I'm not hurt, she thought. Dazed, she looked about her. One of the old mullion windows had blown in, the glass astonishingly intact but hanging drunkenly by the frame. As in slow motion, plaster and dust floated down on the remains

of tables and benches. The window hanging at a crazy
angle swung to and fro from a single hinge, creaking
ominously, and then with a great juddering rattle it fell
to the floor.

A rush of adrenalin and years of training came to
her rescue. She pulled herself up from the floor. She
could almost think straight. There had been an explosion of some kind in, or near, the pub. Jonathan wasn't
answering her; she couldn't see him over the fallen
beam. And, although she herself wasn't hurt, other
people were shouting and screaming, frightened and
obviously in pain.

'Jonathan!' she shouted. No answer. No way over
the table. She slid gently underneath. He was slumped
half beneath the table. There was a long, deep gash on
his forehead which was oozing, not gushing, blood.
Kate found Jonathan's wrist and felt for his pulse. It
was slow, erratic, but strong. She slid a hand beneath
his sweater and felt steady heartbeats. 'Jonathan,' she
spoke directly into his ear. There was no response. She
gently prised open each eyelid, and found both pupils
equal, though staring and unblinking. A steady shower
of dust and plaster trickled down through the join in
the table.

Kate made a swift decision. Gently she pulled him
completely off the bench and down to the comparative
safety of the floor protected by the heavy oak table.
She blew away such dust as she could from his head
wound and tore off her light cotton jacket, tying it
loosely round his head. She tried again to rouse him
without success.

She said into his ear, 'I'm going to get help,
Jonathan, and to see if there's anything I can do. Stay
here; you'll be safe.' She wriggled herself up from
beneath the table, just as another rumble shook the
building and more timbers and walls crumbled about
her.

It seemed hours later before outside help arrived. In fact it was only minutes before passers-by started to do what they could, and the fire-engine moved swiftly down from the station at the top of the High Street while the dust was still settling.

Kate crawled out from beneath the table as the tremors from a second smaller explosion died away. There was a minuscule silence as those trapped or reasonably mobile like herself digested this further shock, then all hell broke loose. People screamed and shouted, and somebody near Kate moaned in obvious pain.

The sound seemed to come from beneath an upturned bench. Kate scrabbled her way over the mound of shattered bricks, glass and mortar, and felt, rather than looked, for the victim. The lights had been extinguished by the first blast, leaving, incredibly, a few flickering candles, romantically lit for effect, casting a wavering light over the debris. Even the second explosion hadn't blown out all the flames.

Kate grabbed a candle from a perilously leaning table and lowered it so that she could see beneath the bench. A young girl lay there, terribly cut about by glass and partly concealed by the body of a young man who was lying diagonally over her. The girl was crying and moaning.

'It's all right,' said Kate in her calm, professional voice. 'I'm a nurse. I'll look after you.'

Her words, she knew, were largely empty promises. What she could do without medical supplies was limited, but at least she could reassure the frightened girl.

'Oh, Nurse, my leg hurts, and Craig—is he all right?'

'Craig's your boyfriend?'

'Yes. But I don't know what's happened to him.'

Kate leaned over and felt for the boy's pulse. Obviously the girl did not realise that he was stretched across her legs. There was no response from the radial pulse. She tried the temporal and plantar pulses without receiving any signs of activity. She found a gap in his torn shirt and felt for a heartbeat. There was nothing. She put her cheek to his mouth to detect the slightest sign of life. There was nothing. Her hands found a huge gash at the back of his head. He was beyond resuscitation. As gently but as firmly as she could she pulled the body off the girl's legs. The girl shrieked and fainted with pain. Clearly she had multiple fractures of bones above and below the knee.

Out of the blue, two strong, tanned hands appeared beside hers, and, in spite of the confined space, lifted the body of the boy off the girl. A deep reassuring voice spoke in her ear. 'Well done, Kate. Let's have a look at this girl.'

Kate could have wept with relief at the sound of Dr Rory North's voice. She nodded her agreement. Somehow, with a calm that later was to astonish her, she told him that she had been unable to find signs of life in the boy Craig, and had concentrated on moving the body to assess the girl's injuries.

Rory dragged his surgical case from behind him. 'Draw up an injection of diamorph,' he instructed, 'and give it to her in her arm. Let's see what we can do about splinting this leg.' He pulled a couple of pieces of broken wood from the pile of rubbish, and found bandages in his case. 'There, that should hold for a bit.' Belatedly he asked, 'Are you all right?'

Kate nodded. 'But please look at Jonathan.' She gestured to the mountain of rubble behind him. 'He's under the table. A head wound, pulse slow and erratic, but pupils equal.'

'Thank God for that; let's have a look at him.'

Kate gave the girl the injection. There was nothing else she could do for the moment. She followed Rory as he scrambled over the pile of bricks and glass.

Jonathan was still unconscious when they reached him, his wound still oozing blood sluggishly.

'Yours?' asked Rory, touching the blood-soaked jacket covering the wound. Kate nodded. Rory lifted a corner of the material. 'OK, that'll do for the moment. Let's have a two ml amp, 1.25mg. Pethilorfan—that should keep things at bay for a while.'

Even as she carried out his instructions, taking the ampoules and syringe from his case, Kate realised that Rory was treating her as well as the injured people. Being able and capable of doing something useful was as necessary to her as pain-killing drugs and bandages were to the more seriously affected victims of the explosion. Other voices, other sounds penetrated, but meant little. The firemen who had arrived earlier were going about their business in a workmanlike fashion; Kate could hear them talking to each other. They were steadily removing fallen beams and other obstructions to reach the injured and the dead.

'There's someone behind the bar in trouble,' Rory said, and she knew that this was the voice that she must obey. 'Let's see what we can do.'

He gave her one hand and took his case in the other. Fallen beams and bricks were piled so high that they were able to walk up the shifting slope to the top of what was left of the bar. The scene behind it was horrifying. Broken bottles had showered down on Jack Beamish, the publican, and the young barmaid who had been on duty. They had both apparently suffered serious injuries in the explosion, and in addition had been badly cut by flying glass.

Jack's face was a mass of blood and exposed bone, and one leg was almost severed just above the knee. Mercifully he was unconscious. Rory gave him a quick superficial examination, though, because his facial injuries were so bad that Rory was unable to properly assess his pupil reaction.

'Cover his face and leg with anything you can find to stop more rubbish falling on to the raw surfaces,' he told Kate.

Miraculously, a pile of clean glass-drying towels were still stacked on a shelf beneath the remains of the bar. Only the top one or two were dirty. Kate took possession of them and spread one over Jack's face and a couple over the torn, mutilated leg.

Rory was examining the barmaid. 'She's only a kid,' he said in a strained voice.

'A student at the college,' Kate explained, 'doing part-time work.' She added, 'She doesn't seem to be too badly hurt.' In fact, except for a couple of superficial cuts on her face and one on her arm, she seemed to have been untouched, and yet she was deeply unconscious.

Rory inspected her eyes. 'Pupils unequal,' he said. 'Must have a head injury.' Together he and Kate carefully turned the inert form. Kate, for all her training, was shocked when she saw a large wedge of thick glass protruding from the back of the girl's head.

'Oh, my God!' ejaculated Rory. The words seemed to be dragged out of him. His eyes met Kate's over the girl's body. She guessed that he didn't readily blaspheme. 'The poor kid must have fallen back on to it. Nothing we can do, except make sure that it stays *in situ* till we can get her to hospital. You stay with her, Kate, keep her on her side. No point in giving her anything as she's out for the count and any pain-killer will only depress her blood-pressure and respirations further.'

There was a jacket hanging drunkenly on a hook above a shelf, and Kate pulled it down and spread it over the girl.

Rory said, 'I'm going back over there, my dear. The ambulance people should be here any minute. I'll get them to take these two first.'

'And Jonathan,' she pleaded.

'If they can, but you know that he's not too bad; he might have to wait. Make sure that whoever escorts these two understands about not touching the glass penetrating the girl's skull, and make sure that they keep her on her side. You'll do that, Kate, won't you?'

She was suddenly angry with herself for even mentioning Jonathan. She knew that what Rory had said was true. He'd a nasty gash on his forehead, and was undoubtedly badly knocked about, but his vital signs were good, and he was not in a life-threatening condition. He could wait for admission to hospital.

Guilt made her retort sharply to Rory's request.

'Of course I'll see that everything's done properly. You can trust me, you know; I am a trained nurse.'

'Of course,' he said gently. 'I never doubted your capabilities.' He raised a smile somehow, which, considering the desolation around them, was miraculous. He climbed back over the bar and disappeared from sight.

Waiting, although it was not long before an ambulance crew arrived, was the hardest thing to do. Kate could hear people crying and calling for help, and felt helpless because she couldn't go to them, although it was quite obvious now that other helpers were at work. But her priority, even if Rory hadn't spelled it out for her, was clear. She must watch over these two badly injured souls until she could hand over to other professionals.

At last a doctor, identified by an accident and emergency jacket and accompanied by two ambulance men, clambered over the debris and squatted down beside her. 'I'll take over, OK?' he said. 'You look as if you could do with a break.'

Kate handed over, but not before repeating Rory's instructions about the girl.

'Will do,' said the young doctor. 'We've already been briefed by his nibs.'

When the pub owner and the barmaid had been taken away, Kate made her way back to the corner table where she and Jonathan had sat eating their ploughman's a lifetime ago.

Jonathan still lay as she and Rory had left him, beneath the table. He was still unconscious, his pulse still slow and sluggish but strong. His wound had stopped bleeding. The police and other emergency services were now in command and there was nothing more she could do for the other victims of the accident.

Kate sat down cross-legged beside him, took his hand in hers, and kept vigil over him.

An unknown time later Rory slid down beside her. His dark-blond hair was covered in a fine white dust, and so were his hands and clothes. He took Jonathan's blood-pressure, checked his eyes again and ran expert hands over his body.

'The ambulance people are coming for him now, Kate,' he murmured. 'Let me run you home to get washed and changed and then I'll take you to the hospital.'

Kate shook her head. 'No, I'm going with him.'

He gave her a look which she didn't even notice. 'I thought you might,' he said wearily. 'Well, at least have a swig of this.' He handed her a small silver hip-flask. 'Purely medicinal.'

'What is it?'

'Brandy.'

'I don't like brandy.'

Even more wearily he said. 'You're not supposed to like it—it's medicine.' He took off the tiny cap and raised the flask, which she still held, to her lips. 'Just take it, doctor's orders.'

She swallowed a mouthful and spluttered and coughed with the effort. Rory grinned at her. 'That's better,' he said. 'You've got some colour in your cheeks.'

The ambulance people arrived and agreed that she could accompany Jonathan to the hospital.

Kate and Rory followed the men with the stretcher out to the door, which was in fact, non-existent. Where the door had been a monster-size hole gaped in the old, thick walls.

A policeman standing by the exit asked Kate to give him her name and address. 'We'll want a statement from you tomorrow, miss,' he started to explain, then broke off and stared hard at Kate. 'I say, it's Sister Christy, isn't it?' Kate nodded. 'Were you here with young Dr North when it happened, Sister?' He jerked his head in the direction of the stretcher-bearers, who were just about to load Jonathan on board.

'Yes,' whispered Kate in a cracked voice.

'I say, I am sorry,' said the young policeman with sincerity. 'Is he badly hurt, do you think?'

Rory intervened in a firm, deep voice. 'We think not too badly, Officer, but we'll know more when we get him to hospital.' He smiled to take any unfriendliness out of his words. 'Now, may I escort Sister to the ambulance? She's going with Dr North to St Just's.'

'Of course, sir—please.' He stood aside so that they could pass.

Outside the road was busy with firemen and ambulance men, and noisy police cars, sirens wailing and blue lamps flashing urgently.

'I'll follow in my car,' said Rory, 'and take you home when you're ready.'

Kate started to protest.

'You're out on your feet,' he replied in a dispassionate voice. 'And we'll both be needed at the centre tomorrow. The sooner you get to bed the better.'

She asked. 'What time is it?'

'Nearly one a.m.'

'Oh, I should let my mother know that I'm all right.' She felt guilty at not having thought of this before.

'Someone has already done that—a neighbour who was near by when the explosion happened. We explained that you were staying to help.'

'Oh, good.' She climbed into the ambulance and sat holding Jonathan's hand.

When they reached the hospital she was asked to wait in the reception area until he had been seen by a doctor and admitted. Eventually she was allowed to see him for a few minutes in Intensive Care, where he had been taken because he was still concussed.

Rory was waiting for her when she left the unit. He put a supportive arm round her shoulders. 'Come on,' he said. 'Home and bed.'

She didn't remember the ten-minute drive home, or saying goodnight to Rowland North, though she did remember him telling her to have a warm shower before going to bed.

Her mother, having been reassured that Kate was all right, was asleep, and so was young Thomas.

Obedient to doctor's orders, she stood under the shower and let the blessedly warm water wash away the dust and dirt and some of the horrors of the evening. Somehow she shampooed her hair and dried it, zombie-like, before falling into bed, to sleep dreamlessly.

CHAPTER THREE

KATE was shattered to find, the next morning, just how affected she was by what had happened. She didn't want to see, or hear, or talk about the events of the previous night. Had it been possible, she would have liked to go into hiding. Common sense told her that this was unrealistic. Not only would the police be in evidence, with their legitimate questions, but television and newspaper reporters as well, scavenging for a story.

To be physically sore and bruised, she had expected, but she hadn't expected to be so emotionally off-balance. To her surprise, her hands were shaky and she was snappy with her mother, who had switched off the TV in her bedroom when she heard Kate coming.

'I'm so sorry, darling Ma,' she said, almost in tears. She gave her mother a hug, and bent again to ease on the support-stockings over Mrs Christy's oedematous feet and ankles.

'It's all right, love—only to be expected after what happened last night.' She stretched out a hand and stroked her daughter's shining hair. 'I'm sorry I was such a damned nuisance yesterday when you got home and wanted to get off for your drink with Jonathan.'

'Oh, Mother, you know you're not a nuisance.' They hugged each other. 'Whatever would I do with myself if I didn't have to muck around with you each day?'

They smiled at each other. It was a standing joke to take the heat out of the situation whenever they became over-emotional—to pretend that Kate wouldn't know what to do with herself if she didn't have her mother to look after.

'By the way, how is Jonathan?' asked Mrs Christy. 'You must both have had your hands full last night, coping with the injured.'

Kate was surprised to find that her mother didn't know about Jonathan, and was full of remorse. She should have told her straight away what had happened, not pushed aside her questions while she helped her shower and dress. It was frustrating enough for the almost house-bound invalid to depend on third-hand reporting without her own daughter clamming up on her.

'Jonathan was injured in the bombing, darling; he's in St Just's.'

'Oh, my dear girl, how awful for you and for Matt, too, with his heart condition. Will it set him back, do you think? And poor Jonathan, I'm so sorry. Is there anything I can do?' She gave an ironic laugh. 'Well, send a card or something. Go to see him. Dora could take me——'

Kate interrupted. 'He's unconscious at present. At least, he was last night. I'm just going to ring the hospital and find out how he is this morning.'

Just how disorientated can you get? she wondered, as she stood waiting to be connected with Intensive Care? She had meant to telephone first thing and enquire about Jonathan, but had, instead, immersed herself in the routine of getting her mother ready for the day. Was it a deep-seated reluctance to hear bad news, or an unconscious but deliberate act of delay? Even that seemed a weird idea to take aboard at this moment. Her job might cause her to analyse people and reactions, but surely she could stop doing it for once?

She spoke sharply to the switchboard operator, who just as sharply answered, 'I'm doing my best; I can't make Intensive Care answer—they're rather busy after last night.'

'Yes, of course they are,' replied Kate, full of regret for being impatient. 'I do apologise.'

The doorbell rang while she stood by the hall table with the receiver in her hand. She prayed that it wouldn't be the police or a reporter.

'I'll go,' said her mother, manoeuvring her wheel-chair along the wide passage.

The locks and door-handles throughout the old house had long ago been moved to positions that Madeleine Christy could manage from her chair, but without tearing the eighteenth-century house to pieces the heavy wooden doors could not be replaced. With an effort, after unlocking the catch, Mrs Christy slowly pulled the door open to reveal Rory North silhouetted against the early-morning sunlight.

Kate, from her position halfway down the hall, saw him framed in the doorway, as in a picture. He almost filled the frame, tall, broad-shouldered, his mane of bronze-blond hair brushed back in a thick wavy mass, like a halo round his leonine head.

'It must be Mrs Christy,' he said, leaning down to shake her mother's hand. 'I'm Rowland North—Rory—and you are a great friend of my Uncle Matthew.' He smiled.

Kate heard her mother saying something just as a voice at the other end of the phone spoke into her ear.

'Sister Hooper, Intensive Care,' said the voice. 'Can I help you?'

Kate explained that she was enquiring about Jonathan.

'Ah, yes,' replied Sister Hooper. 'We've had several calls about Dr North. Are you a relative?'

'No, but I'm. . .' She hesitated. If she said fiancée they would probably be much more forthcoming, but a reluctance to pretend made her say with honesty, 'I'm the managing nurse at the health centre, and a very close friend.'

'Well, he's had a satisfactory and comfortable night,' came the expected reply.

'Is he still unconscious?'

There was a pause, and then the voice said in a tone hovering between the professional and the friendly, 'Yes, though not deeply so. Look, I suggest that you ring again later, say about eleven. The registrar will have done his round then, and there might be more news.' There was an audible, though muffled conversation going on at the other end of the phone, and then Sister Hooper's voice came over clearly. 'That was some of the other staff,' she explained. 'We all want to say how sorry we are about what happened in Midchester. Please give our sympathy to all concerned.'

'Sure, will do,' replied Kate in a throw-away fashion. She put down the receiver.

Rory, having nodded in passing, was following her mother in her wheelchair down the hall towards the big family kitchen.

'Come and have some coffee,' Maddy was saying.

'Just a quick one,' replied Rory in his deep, warm voice. 'Kate and I must get to the surgery in good time.'

Kate, hard on their heels, protested, 'But I'm going to drive in presently as usual. My car wasn't involved last night, you know, and I'm perfectly well able to drive.'

Her nephew Thomas, still in pyjamas, chose that moment to half jump, half fall down the stairs. He stopped dead when he saw a stranger in the house.

'Who are you?' he asked belligerently, staring at Rory.

'I'm Rory North, your aunt Kate's new colleague, a doctor at the health centre.' He held out a hand to the boy.

Kate explained, 'Dr North is a cousin of Jonathan's. He's helping out while old Dr North is ill.'

Thomas continued to stare, ignoring Rory's outstretched hand.

'But what are you doing here now?' he asked in a cross voice.

Rory moved forwards and grasped the boy's right hand. 'There was a bombing last night, in the pub, the Gun and Duck. Did you know about it?'

Thomas shook his head. Maddy spoke. 'He was asleep when Richard Llewellyn came in with the message.'

'Your aunt Kate,' said Rory, sounding very solemn, 'was in the pub when the bombing took place. She was very brave, and, though bruised from having been thrown by the blast from her seat, she went on helping the injured, as a good nurse should.'

Thomas looked at first disbelieving and then with something like admiration at Kate.

'Did you?' he asked. 'Help people who had been hurt?'

'Well, it's my job,' admitted Kate, unsure of Rory North's intentions. There wasn't really any need to expand on the activities of last night. 'Now please go back upstairs and get washed and dressed ready for school.'

Thomas ignored her instructions. 'Was it a big bomb?' he asked, wide-eyed and no longer belligerent. 'Was there a lot of blood about? Did a lot of people get hurt? Did anybody get killed?'

'That's enough, Thomas,' said Maddy firmly. 'Do as Kate says; go and get ready for school.'

A stubborn look came over the boy's face and he clenched his hands into two fists. 'Not till you tell me,' he shouted, and then louder, 'Not till you tell me what happened!'

Maddy looked defeated and Kate angry.

Rory said softly, 'May I make a suggestion?'

Kate was about to say no. Even if he was a paediatrician and an expert with children, the last thing she wanted was for this arrogant stranger to start interfering in her home life. But her mother nodded.

'Please,' she replied. 'Anything that may help.'

To his credit he turned to Kate before doing anything else. 'Kate?' he enquired. 'Do you mind if Thomas and I sort this out together?'

'Would it matter,' she replied, feeling somehow betrayed by her mother's willingness to accept his help, 'what I think?' She rushed out of the kitchen and up the stairs. For some unaccountable reason tears were stinging her eyes.

She heard her mother murmuring in an apologetic manner, and Rory's deep tones saying something reassuring. Then she reached the turning on the stairs and their voices were lost.

Presently, while she was savagely winding up her long hair into a chignon, she heard Thomas and Rory passing her door on the way to Thomas's room. She snatched a navy blue cardigan from her wardrobe and draped it round her shoulders. The sun was shining brilliantly and the temperature was again high, as it had been during the whole of September, but she found that she was shivering.

She bent to kiss her mother. 'Sorry about that,' she said softly. 'Afraid I'm still rather edgy. Please tell Dr North that I'll see him at the centre.'

'Kate,' said Maddy in an agitated voice, 'you're being both rude and ungrateful.' Suddenly she was the stern mother chastising a recalcitrant daughter. 'If you want to be so ill-mannered, you can pass on your own message, for I certainly will not.'

Her lips had set in the manner that Kate knew meant business. Nothing would move her now. 'All right, I'll speak to him myself.' She let herself out through the

kitchen door to the tiny paved courtyard, and crossed
to the garage—a conversion from the old coach-house.

Before she could open the doors a hand descended
on her shoulder. Rory North's hand. To her surprise,
she pondered for a moment on how odd it was that his
hands had already played a large part in their short
acquaintance. The strong hands on the car window
during yesterday's storm, the firm hand grasping hers
in Jonathan's office, and the professional pair of hands
that had made such a welcome appearance in the pub
last night, just when she'd most needed help. And now
a restraining hand.

She shrugged her shoulders away from his fingers
and turned to face him. 'Don't touch me,' she said in a
hard voice. 'I don't want your help to get to work, Dr
North. My God, you are exactly as Jonathan said—
greedy for power over everything and everyone.'

While she was speaking he had moved round her,
and was standing in front of the still locked doors.

'Kate—Sister Christy. . .' His voice sounded tentative, his sea-green eyes had lost their cold expression;
they were almost pleading. 'Look, we're both needed
at the centre today—things are bound to be chaotic
with Jonathan and Uncle Matt away. Dr Lyons will do
her best, and so shall I, but what everyone will need is
your steadying and knowledgeable influence. You're
not really fit to drive, you know, and if it were anyone
else I would medically order time off to recover from
last night. I can't do that—we all need you at the
surgery—but I can see that you get there safely. Please,
my dear, as the top-notch nurse that Uncle Matt raves
about, let me do this small thing.'

After a speech like that Kate really had no choice.
Slowly she followed him to his Lotus, parked in front
of the house. To her surprise, Thomas was already
installed.

'Dora takes Thomas to school,' Kate said in a flat voice.

'We thought, with your permission, today being rather special, that Thomas could be dropped off on our way.'

Kate conceded defeat as graciously as possible. She gave her nephew a tremulous smile. 'OK, Tom, on one condition.'

'What's that?' he asked suspiciously.

'That you do your homework directly you get home tonight and don't play Granny or Dora up. Agreed?'

'OK, agreed,' replied Thomas.

Rory escorted Thomas up the short drive to the front door of the school.

They look just right together, thought Kate. A man like Rory North is just what Thomas needs after losing both his parents. Unbidden came the idea that she had cherished, that Jonathan would fill the role of substitute father. An idea that she had abandoned. There was no rapport between him and Thomas.

The centre, when they reached it, was swarming with policemen, reporters and television crews. Kate had never been so glad of a supportive male arm. Rory seemed suddenly the only capable and responsible person she could depend upon to see her through all the questions with which she was being bombarded.

Somehow Rory steered her through the thrusting line of reporters and cameramen to the door of the centre. With the help of two policemen, he held open the doors and she moved into the comparative quiet of the centre's reception area.

'This is dreadful,' she said. 'How are the patients going to get through.'

One of the policemen, who introduced himself as Inspector Harris, spoke reassuringly. 'Don't you worry, Sister; we'll have them away in a few minutes. But there are a few questions that we need to ask. Do you feel ready to talk to us?'

His kind and understanding attitude made Kate warm to him. He was, after all, only doing his job. 'I'll tell you anything that I can, Inspector,' she replied. 'If it will help.'

'Thank you.' He proceeded to ask her questions about what had happened when the bomb went off, and then, almost casually, asked if she remembered seeing anything unusual, however apparently insignificant. At first she said quite truthfully that no, she hadn't seen or heard anything unusual. Then, to her surprise, under his expert questioning, she recalled seeing a woman come in through the rear door, from the car park, who had looked round quickly, rather surreptitiously, Kate thought, although she wondered if she was imagining this in retrospect. The woman had hurried into the ladies' loo.

'Of course,' she said apologetically, 'people do look a bit embarrassed if they come into the pub to use the Ladies without having a drink. But there are outside conveniences in the car park. How stupid of me—I've only just remembered that.' She looked at the inspector and at Rory, who had stayed with her while she was being questioned. In a shaky voice she said, 'Oh, lord, does that mean that she might have had something to do with the bombing?'

'Not necessarily, Miss Christy,' he replied. 'But it's one of those details that might help.'

He went away soon after this, but warned that he might need to talk to her again.

Slowly during the course of the day the centre began to settle down into something like a normal routine. It was difficult, of course, because in addition to their usual patient list they were inundated with people affected by the bombing.

They were also two doctors short, which put terrific pressure on Rory and Rachel Lyons.

Rachel, newly qualified, was doing her in-practice training. She worked hard and cheerfully, proving that she had the stuff of a fine GP in her. But it was Dr Rowland North—Rory—who kept them all going during the absence of both the old and the young Drs North, and Mike Dolland, the fourth partner, who was on a walking holiday in the Pyrenees.

Rory, for the time being, was the only Dr North in practice. He was a tower of strength.

After the inspector had left and they sat drinking a welcome cup of coffee as they went through the day's list, he asked her to call a staff meeting later in the day. 'Include the cleaning ladies too,' he instructed. 'We'll need all the willing help we can get to weather this particular storm.'

How right he is, thought Kate, looking round the room, having rounded everyone up for the meeting at four-thirty that afternoon. The realisation had come to her during the day that they weren't only talking about cover for two doctors, but also the morale-boosting need that had hit the community.

Rory gave them a pep talk, and the best medicine that they could have, by emphasising the importance of their help and co-operation.

'Dr Lyons,' he explained, 'has asked me to speak for her, as she couldn't spare time from her visits. I feel rather guilty, as the new boy, seeming to take over, but "needs must when the devil drives", as I'm sure you've all heard my uncle say from time to time.'

He had struck the right note—the much loved older doctor was a great one for proverbs. Quite apart from his natural charisma, which Kate reluctantly had to acknowledge, Rory seemed genuinely loath to assume control. He could not disguise, though, his air of authority and medical superiority which made him the obvious person for the job.

'Many of our patients,' he told them, 'will be suffering from the recently recognised phenomenon of community shock, following the bombing.'

The surgery had been full that morning. A few people had turned up out of curiosity, hoping to find out first hand what had happened at the pub and to Dr North junior. But most patients, in addition to those with appointments, had come because they had directly or indirectly been affected by the catastrophe and were distressed physically or emotionally, or both.

Rory, perched on a corner of the desk, addressing the staff, looked strong, virile and dependable. He had no difficulty in keeping their attention. The fact that he had been up late helping with the bomb victims, and out on an early maternity call, seemed to have left him unaffected.

Reluctantly Kate found herself admiring the man. As a paediatric consultant of considerable standing, he had automatically been cushioned by a respectful staff against the head-on difficulties of general practice. Rarely, over recent years, must he have been called out at night, or met patients without preparation; yet last night and today he had risen calmly to both the usual and the unexpected in a GP's day.

He had conducted the morning surgery and made visits as if he had been doing it for years. The patients who had seen him had all been impressed.

'He's got old Dr North's touch,' one elderly lady confided in Kate. She had been a patient when Dr Matthew North had joined the practice just after the war. 'Of course,' she had continued thoughtfully, 'Rory was a nice little boy and a thoroughly nice young man. I always did find it hard to believe the stories that went around about him when he left Midchester.'

Kate, observing and listening to Rory, found it hard

to believe as well. Surely he wasn't the monster that
Jonathan had presented? Even harder to contemplate
was his being a thief. Thinking these thoughts made
her feel disloyal to Jonathan all over again. It was
worse, of course, because he was lying unconscious in
hospital, when he should have been here holding the
fort and proving that he was capable of handling a
crisis.

One of the cleaning ladies, Dot Harrison, was asking
a question. 'Doctor, why are people now so shattered
by bombing or shooting? I was only a kid during the
war, but my family, and others like us, were getting
bad news all the time, and we were being bombed
regular every night. I don't remember my mum or
anyone else going to pieces, even though we were
scared stiff.'

'Interesting point,' replied Rory. 'Other folk have
remarked on this. According to the clever psychology
experts, it's something to do with knowing your enemy
and being geared for bad news. This happened during
the war. Now we don't expect violence because we are
supposed to be at peace.' He smiled at Mrs Harrison.
'I'm no expert, but it seems as likely a reason as any,
don't you think?'

Dot nodded. 'Yes,' she said, 'it kind of makes sense,
I suppose.'

Rory nodded encouragingly. 'Which is why I'm going
to make a suggestion that will, I'm afraid, mean more
work for all of us, but which will hopefully help our
patients who have been affected by what has happened.
I dare say most of you know someone who has been
involved in the affair, apart from our own Jonathan
and Kate, of course.'

There was a hum of agreement. Everyone present
knew of someone affected by what had happened.
Everyone wanted to do as much as possible to help,

but nobody could quite see how this might be achieved. 'What can we do to help?' several people asked.

'How would it be,' suggested Rory, 'if we postponed the Well Woman clinic and the Fit Man sessions for a week or two, and instead have a sort of social get-together? Anyone could come; people might help each other get over what has happened. What do you think?'

He looked round at everyone and there was another ripple of subdued conversation.

'You mean,' said one of the community nurses, 'a sort of do-it-yourself-get-rid-of-your-guilt-or-grief session?'

'Yes,' said Rory, 'you could put it like that. Again, to quote the experts, it seems to be necessary for friends and neighbours of victims to acknowledge their involvement, talk about it, air their feelings.'

Dot Harrison put up a tentative hand. 'Do you mind if I say something again, Doc—sorry—Doctor?'

'Please, feel free.' Rory waved an expansive hand.

'Well, for what it's worth, coming from me and Betty here——' she nodded towards her colleague '—we think it's a good idea what you're suggesting, but don't see where we come in. Well, we only do the cleaning and things, don't we? We're not clever professionals like you lot,' she continued, indicating all and sundry, 'so how can we help?'

'By being here with everyone else. You're both part of the centre. You know a lot of people in the town. The whole object of the exercise is, if you like, togetherness. Sounds a bit sloppy and sentimental, doesn't it? But it's what we're talking about, really. Tea and sympathy perhaps describes it best.'

He grinned. 'And I'm sure that you're both great at tea-making. Look, I've got stacks to do in my office before evening surgery. Can I leave it with you to think about? Let Kate know what you decide.' He slid off

the desk, smiled nicely at everyone and made for old
Dr North's office.

There was a great buzz of conversation after he'd
gone. With one or two reservations, everyone present
thought the idea of a social get-together a good one.
The sooner it could be arranged, the better, was the
general opinion. With the competence that a group of
women geared to running homes and jobs were capable
of, a programme was soon devised, dates fixed, and a
division of labour relating to the provision of food and
drinks worked out.

Miss Potts, usually the odd one out where combined
activity was called for, was for once very eager to prove
herself. It was she who thought of asking patients to
contribute cash towards the event and within minutes
had found and labelled a tin for donations.

'Dr Rory,' she said, doggedly pursuing her course of
being closely linked with the North family, 'emphasised
the fact that people should be made to feel useful.
Well, those who can't do anything else can at least
splash out with cash.'

Kate reflected, as she went to report to Rory, that
even the *idea* of doing something positive had bright-
ened the day that had begun with the staff being
overwhelmed with shock and sorrow. He had been
right about involving everyone, though she'd had her
doubts about asking them to take on a bigger work-
load when they were already stretched.

He'd been right about other things too, like her not
being fit to drive to work; she had been too shaky, too
anxious about Jonathan to concentrate properly. As
the day progressed, and she was forced to push her
own thoughts and feelings into the background, she
had begun to adjust and get control of herself. Now, at
the end of the afternoon, she was almost back to
normal.

Rory North's door was ajar and she could hear him

speaking on the telephone. He sensed that she was there and called for her to enter.

'Enquiring about Jonathan,' he murmured. He listened to something that was being said at the other end. 'Right, thanks.' He put down the receiver. 'No change since mid-morning,' he told her. 'He's still unconscious, for some reason. No known cerebral damage, pulse, BP and temp all OK.' He smiled at her reassuringly. 'Look, he's in good hands. I was talking to a friend at lunchtime—he's a high-flown neurologist. He assured me that this sort of thing is not uncommon under the circumstances. Jonathan might be out for a few days and then recover suddenly. It happens.'

After surgery that evening Rory drove Kate to the hospital. She hadn't the energy or will to refuse his offer of a lift; in fact she was grateful for his company. She managed to quell the niggle of disloyalty to Jonathan, remembering his plea that she shouldn't be taken over by his cousin. So much had happened since then to change the lives of many people in the little market town.

Surely, she thought, as she and Rory stood looking down at his inert body, attached by tubes to an array of display panels, Jonathan would not condemn her for putting herself temporarily into Rory's capable hands? Please, please, she prayed silently, get better soon, darling.

As if knowing what her thoughts were, Rory took her hand in his and squeezed it gently. 'He's going to be all right,' he said. 'He'd be glad to know that you're soldiering on and holding things together at the centre, and,' he added with a grin, 'taking whatever help you can get from whatever source.'

Kate remembered what he had said when she was getting ready for bed. 'Well, whatever else he is,' she said out loud, 'Rory North is a kind and thoughtful man.' And not, she thought as she drifted into sleep, the least bit arrogant deep down.

Considering her first impression of the man and Jonathan's condemnation of him, it was a rather surprising conclusion.

CHAPTER FOUR

JONATHAN regained complete consciousness on the third day following the bombing. Nobody was able to explain why he had remained virtually unconscious for that period. X-rays and examinations seemed to prove that there was no injury responsible for his unconscious state. His facial wound was deep in places, but was satisfactorily repaired by suturing, and healing well. He might have plastic surgery later, if necessary, the surgeon had suggested, but it seemed unlikely that this would be needed.

He looked, Kate thought, seeing his unbandaged face for the first time since the accident, very young and naked without his beard, which had been shaved off. She shied away from the word 'weak', though this had been the first adjective to spring to mind at the sight of his shorn chin.

She was glad that she was there alone to see him so vulnerable. Rory had offered to take her to the hospital as he had for the past three days, but she had refused his offer when the message came through that Jonathan was properly conscious.

Rory hadn't insisted, understanding her need to see his cousin without a third party being present.

'Tell him I'll bring Uncle Matt in to see him later,' he said. 'And don't rush back; we'll just have to manage without you for an hour or so, hard as that may be.'

He gave her an engaging smile that made her wonder how she could ever have imagined him arrogant and unfriendly. His eyes too, sea-green still but softened by golden flecks, were full of warmth and gentleness, all coldness gone from them.

These last few days had been frantically busy for everyone, and yet there had been a subdued air of elation about the centre. A feeling every so often that, in spite of the tragedy that had hit their small town, the comradeship and determination shown by everyone to do their best was a special bonus. An experience that, but for the bombs and the subsequent injuries and deaths, would otherwise have passed them by.

Kate was extraordinarily pleased that Rory should appreciate her efforts and say so. She felt herself, to her annoyance, blushing at his complimentary tone.

Rory's benevolent smile turned to one that was faintly teasing when she blushed. They were in his office. No, old Dr North's office, she reminded herself, although Rory seemed to fill the room with his vibrant personality. Yet somehow, she thought again, he never detracted from the older doctor's reputation. He managed to convey the feeling that he was only holding the fort for his uncle, the true expert in community medicine.

But without him, and with Jonathan in hospital, even with the willing Dr Rachel Lyons they could not have continued. Kate shuddered to think what would have happened without Rory North's presence.

He stretched across the old-fashioned desk and touched her hand. She hoped he hadn't noticed that it trembled beneath his touch. The spot where his fingers rested seemed to burn, to be electrified in a fluttering feather-light manner.

Without a word being spoken, he appeared to have divined all that she was thinking.

'Go and see Jonathan,' he said gently. 'It's you he will be longing to see. And Kate,' he spoke in a slightly hesitant manner, 'don't be surprised if he seems a little strange. Concussion can produce odd reactions.'

She left the centre thinking about what he had said, both about Jonathan and about the part she had played in keeping things going over the last three days.

There was no point in being over-modest about her role. Her knowledge as an administrator and her practical nursing ability had enabled her to guide and support Rory North and Rachel Lyons. While she had relied on them for their medical expertise, and would not have dreamed of overriding them on clinical medical matters, she had been able to smooth their way considerably in the wider aspects of patient care.

The three of them had worked together harmoniously for the benefit of the practice as a whole. Dr Lyons proved over and over again her ability as a general practitioner, making great strides in her understanding of patients seen at the surgery or in their own homes, without the constant back-up of a hospital hierarchy of seniors and consultants to depend upon. When in doubt, she asked for help, either from Kate as manager, when it concerned the after-care treatment of a patient, or from Rory, where diagnosis and treatment were debatable.

In his turn, Rory, without one whit losing his air of authority, confided to Kate that it had been a long time since he'd dealt with patients, 'in the battle zone,' as he put it.

'I'd forgotten, if I ever really knew, what GPs have to cope with,' he said on the second evening following the bomb attack, after a busy surgery. 'My God, no wonder dear old Uncle Matt had a heart attack; I'm not surprised after all these years of caring for patients on a day-to-day basis.'

Kate had said tartly, though sympathising with his sentiments regarding old Dr North, 'Jonathan has done his bit, you know; he has taken on a lot of extra work to spare his father some of the load.'

Rory had looked surprised at her rush to praise Jonathan.

'Well, of course he has. Uncle Matt has made it plain that he couldn't have managed without him. He's to be congratulated on his efforts.'

Nothing in his tone or manner indicated anything but genuine respect for his cousin's work, but for some reason Kate felt uncomfortable on Jonathan's behalf at Rory's expression of commendation.

To further confound her, Rory added, 'I can't wait for Jonathan to get back in harness and steer me through the maze of on-the-spot decisions regarding the best way to deal with an elderly arthritic patient, or the definitive diagnosis for skiving. Somehow, one didn't expect to find the work-shy here, in the affluent south, a stronghold for work, effort and reward.'

Just that last bit had sounded rather tongue-in-cheek, Kate thought later, mulling over what he had said. Sarcastic even, as if he disliked the mainly comfortably-off community in the old market town. Though why he should, when he had private consulting rooms in Harley Street as well as a prestigious post as a paediatric consultant in a large teaching hospital, she couldn't imagine.

She didn't of course, relate any of these feelings to Jonathan when she arrived at his bedside, thrilled to find him conscious and remarkably alert.

'Rory wants you back as soon as possible,' she said softly. 'He's managing with Rachel's help to keep things going, but neither of them knows the ropes as you do.'

She had thought that the knowledge that Rory of all people might need his help would please him, but all he said was, 'Well, he'll have to want on, won't he? I'm nowhere near fit enough to work at present, nor will I be for some time yet.'

Not only his words but the bitterness with which he'd

uttered them struck Kate like a blow. For some reason she'd thought that he would be longing to get back to the practice.

'Oh, darling,' she said contritely, 'no one wants to rush you, it's just that everyone's looking forward to having you back. We miss you.' She bent to kiss him and pat his hand comfortingly, much as she would have reassured her nephew Thomas under similar circumstances.

The unit sister came over to have a word at that point. 'You must be pleased with Dr North's progress,' she said to Kate. 'We'll be turfing him out tomorrow.'

Jonathan protested in a horrified voice, 'But I'm not ready to go home, Sister. Good lord, I only regained consciousness a few hours ago.'

'Oh, no, Doctor, you won't be going home for a day or two, but you don't need to stay here in IU; you're being moved to a side ward on Men's Medical.'

Kate had been surprised by Jonathan's outburst. Even if he wasn't well enough to be discharged, she couldn't help feeling that it would be natural for him to want to go home. After all, most patients were only too ready to leave hospital provided that they had a good home to go to. It was usually only the poor or lonely elderly folk who were reluctant to leave the shelter of hospital.

Though she felt surprised, she didn't show it. Years of training enabled her to conceal her feelings; but Jonathan's reaction bothered her. It seemed strange that he shouldn't be champing at the bit, longing to get back to Midchester, even if he wasn't well enough to start work. He had a large and comfortable flat of his own in the old manor house that had belonged to the Norths for generations. His one-time nanny, Mrs Crump, now housekeeper, doted on him and would spoil him rotten. He had every reason to want to go home.

They talked a little more, or rather Kate did. She tried to convince herself that Jonathan's sulky silence was on account of his recent unconsciousness, but in her heart she knew that this wasn't the reason. He seemed almost indifferent to her presence and, when she told him that Rory was bringing his father in for a visit, he muttered, turning his head away from her, 'Tell him not to bother,' and then, as if sensing her hurt bewilderment at his words, added, 'But give Dad my love and tell him not to worry about me.'

Kate left a little while later, kissing him with all the warmth that she could muster, and reassuring him repeatedly that he was needed at home and at the centre, but that everyone would understand that he wasn't well enough to work yet.

To her surprise, the unit sister followed her out to the waiting area outside Intensive Care. She looked determined but a little uncomfortable.

'I know,' she began cautiously, 'that you are more or less engaged to Dr North, as well as being the manager at the health centre. I wonder, can you tell me if anything was, or is, troubling him, apart from the shock and injury that he sustained in the bombing?'

Kate was even more surprised by her question, finding it difficult to imagine what the other nurse was thinking about in clinical terms.

'Well, no, not really,' she replied weakly, aware that her response was totally inadequate. 'Why, is there something wrong that we don't know about? Look, Dr North's father and his cousin, both doctors, are coming in later; perhaps you should talk to them.'

'Oh, yes, Miss Christy, I will do that; but we felt that you might have more information about the patient, as well as more influence over him.'

'Yes, perhaps, I'll think about it. If there is anything, I'll tell you.' Kate was ashamed of feeling and sounding so vague. What was the competent sister of the intensive care unit trying to find out? It almost sounded as if she and the medical staff were more bothered about Jonathan's mental or emotional state than his physical condition. Obviously everyone concerned had been somewhat surprised that he hadn't regained consciousness sooner. Were they suggesting that there was some sinister reason for his prolonged unconscious condition?

From having been uplifted and excited by the news of Jonathan's improvement, Kate now felt exhausted. All she wanted at this moment was to go home and be spoiled by her mother. Suddenly she felt like a child in need of care and undemanding love. At first she thought that only her mother could supply this, her physical disability in no way impairing her strength of character or ability to be strong and supportive.

Then out of the blue came a picture of Rory North, tall, broad, blond, rather like a picture of a noble warrior, a Viking in a child's book but, beneath the solid, handsome physique, a dependable, assured, kindly person. She thought of his hand upon hers, and the 'electricity' that had passed between them. She needed his strength and support to weather this particular storm.

She sat in her car and mechanically fastened the seatbelt. 'Oh, Rory,' she muttered. 'Please help me.'

Carefully, but in a daze, feeling as shaky as she had the day after the explosion, she drove the twelve miles back to Midchester. She diverted on the way to call in at the old manor house and report to Dr North on Jonathan's condition.

He was sitting in the shade on the terrace, still looking frail, but less anxious than when she had last seen him on the day following the bombing.

'I wanted to go and sit with my boy, you know, and so did Crumpy, but the hospital advised against it. We went in yesterday several times, and the day before, but all the clever boffins there didn't think that it would help if we stayed. Of course, I could have insisted, but one has to accept that these folk know what they are doing.'

'Yes, I wanted to stay, but they said it would be better to let him return to consciousness naturally. They didn't seem to have any doubts about his recovery, and they were right, of course. He's going to be moved to a side ward on Men's Medical tomorrow and will probably be home in a couple of days.'

'You're a good girl, Kate.' Old Dr North gave her a sidelong look, very sharp and knowing. 'Too good for Jonathan.' His chuckle took the edge off his words. 'As I've told him often enough. He should snatch you up while he's got the chance.'

The old man patted her hand and she leaned over to kiss his cheek.

'I must go,' she said. 'I've heaps to do at the centre. We're rather busy, you know, without Doctors North major and minor.' She smiled to show that she was partly joking, and not reminding him of his absence.

'And what about Dr North, medias?' he asked, giving Kate a twinkling smile that reminded her of his nephew rather than his son.

'Rory? Oh, he's quite useful,' she replied with a cheerful giggle. 'Rather grand, of course, being a consultant.' Without her knowing it, her voice softened as she said gently, 'But very willing to learn.'

It was mid-afternoon when she arrived at the centre and found the waiting-room filling up for the mothers and babies clinic. The weather had turned hot and humid again and several of the babies were obviously finding the heat trying and were grizzly and miserable.

Kate, giving everyone a nice cheerful smile as she went through to her office, thought, rather grimly, that the infants reflected her feelings at this moment—at odds with the world. 'I could burst into tears at the drop of a hat,' she muttered savagely to herself.

She realised that she hadn't had any lunch, but didn't feel hungry, only very thirsty. She went along to the little staff kitchen to fetch a glass of water, deciding that she hadn't even got the energy to make tea or coffee.

Rory was seeing a patient out of his room down the corridor and spotted her.

'Kate, come and tell me how you found Jonathan,' he called in a soft voice.

Some sixth sense told her that if she saw Rory now her unshed tears would spill over. Much as she had wanted comforting when she left the hospital, and Rory himself had figured in the role of comforter, she knew that she couldn't talk to him about Jonathan. In spite of the rapport that had developed work-wise between her and Rory, and her need to try to understand Jonathan's strange behaviour, his cousin, whom he so disliked, must be the last person with whom she should discuss Jonathan's weaknesses. It would be sheer treachery to the man she expected to marry.

She reminded herself that it wasn't many minutes before all hell had broken loose at the pub that Jonathan had begged her not to be taken in by his cousin's airs and graces. He had been convinced that Rory had only come to Midchester for what he could get, and that everyone would fall for his charms and be manipulated by him for his own ends.

Kate no longer believed this. She had seen enough of the real man concealed behind the handsome exterior to know that his concern for his uncle, the practice and patients, was absolutely genuine. She was certain that he didn't bear a grudge against Jonathan, or the people of Midchester, for whatever they might have held against him when he'd left his uncle's home twenty years before.

It was amazing how rapidly all these thoughts raced through her mind in the fraction of time that it took Rory to call out.

'Can't now,' she replied. 'Lots to do; I'll see you later. But I've seen Dr North and filled him in.'

In the dim corridor running the length of the building she couldn't see Rory's face clearly, but the way that he dropped his hand, with which he had signalled her, seemed to indicate a shrug of acceptance. He turned back into his office after calling through to the waiting-room for his next patient.

Resolutely, Kate closed her mind to her personal problems and set to to deal with some paperwork before seeing her first patient in half an hour's time. For a moment, the centre was running according to schedule, with the baby clinic supervised by Jan Richards, an experienced midwife, guiding Dr Lyons through the post-natal examinations. Rory was seeing his afternoon appointments—a mixture of special assessments and insurance physicals.

Things might almost have been back to normal.

Her phone rang. It was the police. They had had another description of a woman who might be the person whom Kate had seen coming in from the car park at the pub; could they come and speak to her again? The sooner the better.

'Well, in an hour's time,' agreed Kate wearily, 'I shall be busy this evening.'

The centre was to have the first self-help social meeting that evening. After all the time and effort put into arranging it, she wasn't going to miss being there. Astonishingly, she found herself looking forward to meeting people who might have been in the pub when she and Jonathan were there. It was difficult to see herself as one of those affected by what had happened.

Being a professional on whom others relied made it near impossible to think of oneself as a victim. But rationally, when she came to consider the matter, that was exactly what she was—as much a victim as anyone else.

Only by the fact that she had been able, through training and professional status, to make some contribution to the relief of the injured had she managed to ease her own shock at what had happened. Dimly she had been aware of this on the night of the tragedy, and since then, in small flashes, she had realised that it was a privilege to be involved in the rehabilitation of the injured or the shocked relatives.

How much harder, she could now acknowledge, was the role of relatives who were involved but unable to offer practical help. It didn't bear thinking about. No wonder they needed this kind of community counselling, and how wise Rory had been to suggest such a self-help group. If she was looking forward to meeting others closely involved with what had happened, how much more must those on the fringes welcome the opportunity to talk about their fears and distress?

The idea brought her up hard against a thought that had been hovering in the back of her mind for the past three days, but which she had succeeded in squashing. How did her own mother really feel about what had happened? To please Kate, she had asked only a minimum of questions about that night, since her daughter had made it plain that she didn't really want to discuss the matter.

Now, Kate suddenly realised how unkind this had been. Her mother must have been longing to know from her own lips what had happened, how she'd felt when the bombs exploded and Jonathan had been injured. It wasn't just idle or base curiosity that made her, or any other friend or relative, want to know the

details of the disaster. It was a deep desire to participate as far as possible in a loved one's brush with
death.

Kate decided that her mother must have a chance to
come to the meeting tonight if she wished. She understood now why she had rather wistfully suggested
sending cakes or something along for the refreshment
table.

Mrs Christy, in reply to Kate's phone call, said, 'Yes,
I would like to come,' and added in a rather tremulous
voice, 'Thank you for thinking of me, darling. I'll make
myself useful if I can.'

Kate was still nursing the receiver and wondering
how she could have been so stupid about her mother's
feelings, when there was a knock at the door, and Rory
entered.

'Sorry, are you about to make a call?' he asked.

Kate shook her head. 'No, I've just finished. I was
asking my mother if she would like to come to the
meeting tonight.'

He looked pleased and surprised.

'Well, that's great; I thought that I would bring
Uncle Matt here on the way back from visiting
Jonathan. Good therapy. He'll feel useful chatting to
his own patients. Might make him feel better about
things and I'm sure that they'll all appreciate seeing
him. He'll be no end bucked if your mother is going to
be here too. Can I pick her up on the way?'

'No, thanks, I'm going back to get changed presently, and get Thomas organised for the evening. He
tends to play Dora up when Mother's out.'

'Dora—she's your housekeeper, isn't she?'

'Dora's everything,' Kate explained. 'Friend, companion, nanny, cook, housekeeper. I can't imagine life
without Dora. She's been around since I was a child.'

'Ah, rather like our Nanny Crump. She can't wait to
get Jonathan back home and spoil him to death. Which

is why I've come to have a word. How did you find him—bright, alert? I understood from the registrar who phoned earlier that he was almost back to normal.'

To her horror, Kate felt her eyes fill with the tears that had been threatening since she'd left the hospital. She dropped her head and pretended to be shuffling some papers. He mustn't see her crying, Rory above all people. It seemed desperately important that he shouldn't. Her mind scrabbled around for a satisfactory reason, and came up with the same one that she had worked out earlier. Jonathan's paranoiac dislike for his cousin made it impossible for her to reveal Jonathan's vulnerability to Rory.

She raised her head and blinked back the tears, giving him a watery smile, and then lifted a hand to one eye, hoping to deceive him.

'Something in your eye?' asked Rory, sounding genuinely sympathetic. 'May I?' Without waiting for her to reply, he moved over and stood behind her. 'This one——?' He indicated her right eye.

Kate nodded. He put a hand under her chin and tilted her head further back. 'Now,' he said softly, parting her right eyelids, 'look up.' Kate did, and her left eye involuntarily mimicked the right. She found herself staring up from her dark brown hazel eyes into his—gold-flecked, sea green.

They both froze statue-like, he staring down at her, she up at him. The room was ghostly quiet. Time stood still. Kate was aware of his fingers, feather-light, releasing her eyelids and sliding down her cheek, beneath her chin, and down the stretched column of her throat. Everything was suspended in that moment; even their breathing seemed to stop.

'Oh, Kate,' Rory murmured from a distance.

Slowly she expelled her held breath. 'Rory?' There was a question mark in her husky voice.

'Kate, my dearest dear.' He moved round her chair

so that they were facing each other. His hands cupped her face for a moment, and then slid to her shoulders. Slowly he lowered his own face, until an inch or so above hers. She could smell his aftershave, a delicate, sharp scent, and see the beginnings of a five o'clock shadow on his chin, such a strong chin. Funny, she thought, his beard's quite dark, considering the blondness of his hair.

'Kate?' His voice now was asking a question. He wants to know whether to kiss me or not, she thought.

The telephone on her desk shrilled urgently. They jerked apart as if on elastic bands. The phone continued to ring. Kate took several deep breaths, but she couldn't drag her eyes away from Rory's face.

He straightened up. 'I'm so sorry,' he said, 'so very sorry.' He picked up the receiver and handed it to her.

Like an automaton Kate accepted it from him. Still staring at Rory, she spoke into the phone. 'Yes, yes, I'm ready; please ask the first patient to come in.'

Rory moved towards the door. 'I'll see you this evening,' he said, and she thought that his voice sounded as firm as usual. 'At the bun-fight.' His mouth curved into a sardonic grin. 'Saved by the bell, Kate, yes?'

'Yes.'

There was a tap at the door, and Rory flung it open. The Allen family appeared, all four of them.

'We've come for our late holiday jabs, Sister,' said Mr Allen.

Rory slipped past the Allens through the doorway

'See you tonight, Sister,' he said. With a smile, he disappeared.

CHAPTER FIVE

WITH a tremendous effort, Kate managed to blot out what had just happened between her and Rory, and attend to her patients.

First the Allens, bubbling over with excitement at the thought of their coming safari in Kenya and Tanzania. She gave them their necessary shots and asked them to send her a postcard.

'Oh, we will, Sister, of course, and come and show you our photographs when we get back,' they assured her happily.

Kate wished them a happy holiday and collected her next patient from the waiting-room—a sad, elderly lady who lived alone in a rather run-down semi on the outskirts of the town. She needed a new dressing on a nasty leg ulcer, which was proving slow to heal.

'I could ask the community nurse to call and do this for you,' suggested Kate. 'To save you the trip in twice a week. You're going to need several more treatments yet.'

'Is that what you want me to do, Sister; would it be more convenient for you?' asked Mrs Mawby.

'Good heavens, it makes no difference to me, Mrs Mawby. It's your convenience I'm thinking about, having to get a bus in and perhaps wait for one going back your way.'

'If it's all the same to you, Sister, I'll carry on coming to the centre. It makes somewhere to go, you see. Gives me a reason for going out. I don't know anyone in Midchester. My husband and I only moved here a few weeks before he died. We were going to do such a lot to the house. Now. . .' She spread her hands in a gesture of despair.

Kate could have wept for her. In fact, she thought, it's a day for weeping. A picture of Jonathan looking helpless flashed into her mind.

Making a determined effort to pull herself together, she tried to get Mrs Mawby to talk about her late husband and any relatives or friends that she might have elsewhere. It seemed that the Mawbys were a childless couple, and themselves only children, leaving them with a scattering of cousins with whom they were in contact.

As for friends, they had a few in the town up north where they had lived, but they were mostly elderly and not too mobile. Mr Mawby had been considerably older than his wife, who was in her early sixties. However, she seemed older, walking badly on account of her ulcer, which added years to her posture. Kate also had the impression that she had let herself go recently. She was quite a pretty lady, but devoid of make-up, and her almost snow-white hair was strained back into an unbecoming bun.

Kate had a sudden idea. 'I don't suppose you knew anyone connected with the bombing at the pub?' she asked Mrs Mawby.

'Well, not really, but my milkman lost a friend that night. Poor man, he was in a dreadful state when he delivered the milk the next morning. I made him come in and have a cup of tea. He seemed quite pleased to be able to talk about it.'

Bingo! thought Kate. 'Mrs Mawby,' she said, 'are you doing anything this evening?'

For the first time since meeting her, Kate heard Mrs Mawby laugh. 'I should be so lucky,' she replied.

'Would you be willing to come back in a couple of hours' time and give a hand with our self-help evening?' asked Kate. 'We've invited all our patients and anyone who was affected by the bombing to call in and chat, have a coffee or something. We'd be glad of extra help.'

For a moment Mrs Mawby looked doubtful. 'Wouldn't your regulars mind?' she asked. 'A newcomer butting in?'

'I don't know,' replied Kate honestly. 'But I think you can offer enough through your own experience to justify being here.'

'I shan't go home,' said Mrs Mawby, looking at once animated and years younger. 'I'll go and have some tea at that café by the river. What time do you want me to come back, Sister?'

'Just before eight o'clock. That's when the doors open, as it were.'

'Right, I'll be here, and I won't let you down, I promise.'

Kate, surprised at herself for taking such a strong decision on the spur of the moment, prayed, as she saw Mrs Mawby out and the next patient in, that she hadn't made a colossal mistake. Much as she wanted to help Mrs Mawby, she would normally have considered making such a suggestion with caution. Would any of the staff object to a stranger being invited to participate, or would they understand that she was offering a lifeline to somebody in distress? Surely other people who had suffered shock and deprivation through loss needed support as much as the bomb victims! Well, Mrs Mawby certainly did. She was quite alone, and wouldn't, Kate felt sure, have come to the self-help evening on her own account. She was someone who needed to feel needed. By suggesting that she helped out, Kate had succeeded in getting her to attend.

It was while she was seeing her next and last patient that the police arrived. They were in the waiting-room when she showed Alec Downs, an obese patient coming for a check-up on weight and diet, out of the clinic-room behind her office.

The inspector and sergeant who followed her through to her room were new to her. They went over yet again her description of the woman who had walked through the pub from the car park. 'We've had another description,' they explained, 'and need to compare it with yours, Miss Christy.'

They left fifteen minutes later, reassuring her that they had for the moment got all the information that they needed, but warning that they might call again.

Mechanically she tidied up the clinic and her desk. Now that she had finished work details of the extra-ordinary incident that had occurred with Rory, just before the Allens had arrived, flooded back.

She went hot at the recollection and stared into the small mirror on the wall. She felt different and was surprised that nothing in her physical appearance had changed. Her hazel eyes, topped by smudges of straight brows, still stared back at her from oval face. Her hair, astonishingly, was still neatly coiled into the chignon that she favoured for work. Rory hadn't displaced a single strand of chestnut hair when he tilted her head backwards to examine her eye.

The memory of his hands on her face and neck, and the timeless look that they had exchanged, made her feel quite breathless. She sat down with a bump on her chair. I must pull myself together, she told herself. I mustn't let him see how much it affected me.

He had spoken very casually when the Allens had arrived, as if nothing of note had happened. Well, two could play at that game. She knew that he had already left the building to collect his uncle and take him to St Just's to see Jonathan. There would be no need to face him until they met at the centre later in the evening. By then, she vowed, she would be in full control.

* * *

Kate brought her mother back to the centre just before eight o'clock. She had sorted Thomas out and left him seeming quite happy, for once, to play junior Scrabble with Dora. He had done his homework and agreed to go to bed at eight-thirty, without argument.

'I don't know what's got into Thomas,' Kate confided to Mrs Christy as they motored to the centre. 'He seems more accessible to reason lately. Not that I'm complaining; it's just strange, that's all, don't you think?'

'I think that Rory is having a good influence on him,' said her mother.

'Rory? What has he got to do with it?'

Mrs Christy looked surprised and a little uncomfortable. 'I don't know, really. It's just that Thomas seems to have taken to him, and whenever he's called in they've talked and seemed to have got on well together.'

They arrived at the centre. Kate, shocked by the news that Rory had apparently visited her home without her knowledge, asked between clenched teeth, 'How often has the clever Dr Rory North called in?'

'Well,' Mrs Christy sounded confused, 'only two or three times. Darling, I thought that you knew or, anyway, that you wouldn't mind. Does it matter? He's been so sweet to Thomas. He seems to understand him.'

Kate got the wheelchair out from the boot in silence. Several cars arrived in the car park. Patients and staff called greetings. Somebody came over and helped Kate's mother into her wheelchair and began wheeling her towards the building.

Kate followed behind making a thing about locking the car doors to walk on her own. Clever Rory North, she thought, buttering up my mother, being oh, so nice to Thomas, and to think that I nearly let him. . . She pushed away the memory of the incident in the office;

she wished with all her heart that it hadn't happened. Thank God the phone had rung and she'd been so busy afterwards that she'd not had time to dwell on it. What on earth had happened to her to let him even suppose for one minute that she would allow him to kiss her? What indeed? she asked herself sardonically.

Jonathan had been right after all. No wonder he'd been afraid of her being taken over by his cousin. And she had been happy to reassure him. Of course she wasn't and never would be attracted to the handsome Rory. Jonathan could be sure of her love for him. Nothing serious had happened this afternoon, she reminded herself; at worst it had been an exchange of chemistry. She almost laughed—a chemical reaction, test tubes and Bunsen burner stuff, brought about because she had had a trying morning and was a bit overwrought. Even if the phone hadn't rung, she would not have allowed Rory to kiss her. Of course she wouldn't.

She felt better now, and could even pretend that she didn't much mind Rory's having visited her mother unknown to her.

She pushed through the glass doors to the reception area. A lot of people were already there. Rory's experimental evening had begun.

He, with his uncle, Dr North senior, was standing in the middle of the room, a head taller than anybody else.

Mrs Mawby arrived at that moment, and Kate explained her presence to some of the staff. Dot Harrison took her under her wing. It looked as if the evening would be a success.

Rory came over and stood beside Kate. 'You look stunning,' he said. 'That colour suits you.' He was referring to the russet-coloured angora sweater she was wearing. She knew that it complemented the chestnut-brown column of straight hair that cascaded down her back. His comment surprised her. She had thought that he would be impersonal, professional, distancing himself from the incident in her office.

She said abruptly, 'Why have you been calling at my home over the last few days without telling me?'

He didn't hesitate. 'Because we've been busy, because my visits to "Bathurst" and your mother have all been in passing, never planned.'

She stared at him. He was all that Jonathan had described, all that he had feared. He was doing what Jonathan had predicted, charming everyone, convincing them that he was noble and good. Tall, bronze-blond, handsome, with a quicksilver tongue that could entrap anyone, just as a spider trapped flies in a web.

Kate looked up at him as they stood in the corner of the room, partly screened by the reception desk. She didn't want to think of what Jonathan had said about his cousin, but, having just learned from her mother that Rory had visited her home without her knowledge, she felt at least permitted to question him.

'Busy, my foot!' she exclaimed. 'If you'd wanted to tell me, you could have.'

'Yes, that's true, Kate, but you would have questioned my reasons for visiting, wouldn't you, just as you are questioning them now?'

'But it would have been more honest.'

'Surely, but isn't it your mother's house at least as much as yours? Isn't she allowed to dictate who visits or who does not, just as much as you? Or should she, because she has lost the use of her legs, ask your permission as to whom she allows into the house?'

Kate was shocked. 'You know that I don't believe that.'

'No, of course you don't, but, Kate, you have been responsible for the health and well-being of your mother and Thomas for so long that you feel it necessary to make choices for them at all times.' He put a hand on her arm, and it burned through the wool of her sweater. 'But, my dear, that's not fair to them, or to you. You shouldn't have to shoulder that burden. You should be out having fun when you're not working. Your job's hard enough; you need a break from responsibility occasionally.'

This understanding of her situation took Kate's breath away. She knew that all the things Jonathan had said about Rory were not true, however much she would have liked to believe them for Jonathan's sake. She'd already seen that he was not the devious man of double standards that Jonathan had presented. But, just for an instant, she wondered if the good-looking man before her was in fact capable of manipulating situations for his own ends.

Certainly her mother, together with almost everyone else in the room, was *sold* on him, both as a man and a doctor. She couldn't go along with all that Jonathan had said about his cousin, but a small part of her wondered if Rory weren't a bit too perfect.

True, the exceptional circumstances arising out of the bombing had catapulted Rory and all of them into an unreal situation, forcing him to use all his professional and social attributes to the full. It was as if some uncontrollable force had made sure that he had a chance to demonstrate his authority and charisma. Would he have seemed such a strong, likeable and dependable person if chance hadn't thrown down the gauntlet?

Under more normal circumstances, perhaps he would have seemed simply pushy and too clever by half, as Jonathan had suggested. That was a nonsense, she knew. He was what he seemed to be, a kind, generous and powerful man in the best possible way, using his pursuasive powers and influence for the benefit of those in need. Who else, in a few days, could have got together all these people who were here tonight?

Who else would have tried? Not Jonathan, that's for sure, said a small, treacherous voice in her head.

She took a sip of coffee and choked on it. Rory patted her back. 'All right?' he asked. His eyes held an amused as well as gentle expression.

Kate nodded. 'Yes, thanks.' She smiled ruefully at him. 'Am I really as bossy as you make me sound?' she asked.

'I didn't say that you were bossy, just too concerned for everyone else. Too over-protective of certain people.'

She thought, He means Jonathan as well as Mummy and Thomas.

'People I care about, people I love,' she said quietly, deliberately.

'No one would argue with that,' he replied. And then, as an afterthought, 'By the way, Jonathan was very pleased to see his father; they've already moved him to Men's Medical. There was no reason to keep him in IU tonight.'

'Oh, I'm so glad. He should be home soon. It'll be marvellous to have him back, even if he isn't well enough to work for a bit.' She uttered the words defiantly, as if expecting him to challenge her, and then remembered that Rory didn't know anything of Jonathan's reluctance to return home. She wondered if the unit sister had said anything to him or to Dr North senior about Jonathan.

'Did you speak to the sister?' she asked.

'Just a brief word. I don't think that there are any complications. Jonathan should be quite fit in a short while.' He gave her a reassuring smile. 'Of course, there is bound to be some emotional trauma.' He waved an arm around to indicate the throng of people.

'After all, that's what this is all about, Kate, isn't it—
trauma of the soul and spirit as well as the body?'

Her hand shook, and she spilled some coffee from
the mug she was holding. 'Here,' offered Rory, 'let me
take it.' He removed the mug from her hand, set it on
the counter, and whipped a snow-white handkerchief
from his pocket. 'Allow me,' he said. Without waiting
for her to reply, he began mopping off the trickle of
liquid that had splashed on her wrist.

His long, strong fingers held her hand as he wiped
away at the coffee. His bronze-blond head was bent
near her own. 'Kate, my dear, I'm so sorry about this
afternoon. I shouldn't have been so clumsy. Please
ignore what happened.'

From somewhere she found the strength to say, 'But
nothing happened, Rory, nothing at all that mattered,
did it?' She made herself look straight into his sea-
green eyes, and resisted a desire to touch his cheek.
He must have found time to shave since their encounter, for his cheeks and chin were smooth and innocent
of stubble.

If Rory was surprised by her words, spoken in what
she hoped was a steady, unemotional voice, he didn't
reveal it. He simply smiled, tucked his soiled hanky
away in his pocket, took her arm, and guided her over
to where her mother and his Uncle Matt sat talking to
a group of people.

Among the little crowd gathered round Mrs Christy
and Dr North were a reporter and photographer from
the local weekly paper. They detached themselves from
the group when Rory and Kate approached.

'Oh, no,' said Kate. 'What are they doing here?'

'Their job,' replied Rory. 'The editor rang to ask if
they could cover the event. I did a deal with them.
They've got an exclusive and can sell to other locals or
whoever. It means we won't be inundated with other
newspeople.'

'Well, that was high-handed of you. Don't you think that you should have asked the rest of us what we thought about the Press coming?' She was very angry, and added without really meaning it, 'We're not all of us out to seek publicity, you know.' It was a silly, childish remark to make, and she regretted it immediately. But she couldn't retract it as the reporter met up with them at that moment.

'Hello, Doctor, Sister,' he said pleasantly. 'Thank you for letting us come. We've only just arrived.'

They had been well briefed by their editor, who had agreed with Rory that they would be very circumspect in their dealings with those present. No one would be pressed who was at all reluctant to be interviewed or photographed.

'We do hope that you and the other staff will talk to us,' said the reporter. 'We think that this idea of a sharing-grief group is marvellous.'

The fact that Rory had been so careful when making arrangements with the paper proved, if proof were needed, thought Kate, what a thoughtful and caring man he was. She felt even worse about what she had said. 'Sorry,' she whispered when the opportunity arose a little later. 'I didn't mean what I said about publicity. It was stupid of me.'

'Don't worry about it, Kate.' Rory gave her arm a gentle squeeze before turning to speak to a patient who wanted a word with him.

Soon after that they were parted, each going their separate ways to converse with the many patients and visitors who wanted to speak with them. There had been three deaths and ten people injured at the pub, and, though nobody had come from the bereaved families—it was too soon for that—several relatives of those injured were there. Also present were others who, like Kate, had escaped virtually unhurt. Like her, though, they had been shocked and found it a relief to talk about their feelings.

One of them said, 'I envy you, Sister; at least you were able to do something that night to help. I just felt so bloody useless. Everyone ought to learn first aid or just basic dos and don'ts when someone is hurt. I was more afraid of doing harm by doing the wrong thing.'

Somebody else said, 'Come on, Sister, why don't you and that gorgeous new doctor start classes?'

Kate prevaricated at the time, but later she wondered if it might be possible to incorporate some practical information into their meetings. Not necessarily first aid as such—both the Red Cross and St John's held classes at times—but, as that one person had suggested, enough information to know what to do or not to do.

She would discuss the possibility with Rory. She was too preoccupied with what was going on to realise the irony of her thoughts. A short while ago nothing would have persuaded her to involve him in any project that might require their combined effort; now she was planning to enlist his help in just such a plan.

The evening at last came to an end. It had been a total success. Mrs Mawby came to say goodbye to Kate, just as Rory joined her. 'I can't thank you enough, Sister—I've had a lovely evening,' said that lady, close to tears. 'I know that it must sound odd saying such a thing on an occasion like this, but I've met some lovely people—Dot Harrison for one, and a couple who live in the next street to me. They're giving me a lift home. Thank you so much—can I come to the next meeting and help?'

'We won't be able to manage without you,' replied Kate with a smile.

'Oh, you are a dear,' said Mrs Mawby.

Rory murmured something, which sounded like, 'I second that,' but it was said so softly that Kate couldn't be sure. She turned to look at him, standing calm and rock-like beside her, looking, as always, incredibly handsome. But there was nothing in the innocent gaze that he turned upon her to reject or confirm her suspicions.

His bleeper sounded at that moment. 'Rachel, probably,' he said. He moved and picked up the receiver on the reception desk. He had been right—it was young Dr Lyons on the phone.

Rory had a few words with her and then returned to Kate's side. 'I'll have to go shortly,' he told her. 'A couple of calls have just come in.'

'Are you doing night calls?' Kate asked, surprised.

'Yes, Rachel didn't want to come to the shindig tonight. Do you know that she's a terribly shy person? We agreed to switch duties.'

For the umpteenth time that day Kate felt breathless. Here was this man, yet again demonstrating that he was kind and thoughtful, whatever story he invented to cover the fact that he was doing night calls. What a remarkable person he was.

He left soon after this incident, taking his Uncle Matt home on the way. When everything was tidied up, Kate left with her mother and drove home under a sky full of stars and a harvest moon.

Mrs Christy said, unknowingly virtually echoing Mrs Mawby's words, 'I've had a wonderful evening, Kate. It was splendid seeing so many old friends, although the occasion was a sad one. Matt was pleased too. It did him good, knowing that his patients still hold him in high regard and are looking forward to his return. We must have him over soon for supper. And Rory, of course.'

'Yes, that would be lovely.'

Her thoughts meandered about during the rest of the drive home—in much the same way as her emotions

had see-sawed throughout the last few days—over
Rory North. At times she had been ready to condemn
him as the charlatan whom Jonathan had implied
existed; at times she had been willing to accept the
man with the caring qualities that had been frighten-
ingly perfect.

Only much later, getting ready for bed, did Kate
think constructively of Jonathan. He should be the
one, she decided, whom her mother invited for supper
with old Dr North. Not the oh, so perfect nephew
Rory.

Poor darling Jonathan, she thought, as she drifted
into sleep. What an act to follow.

CHAPTER SIX

THREE days after the special evening at the centre, Jonathan returned home.

Everyone was looking forward to his return for varying reasons. Kate's feelings were mixed and as a consequence she felt guilty.

Her first thought should have been the pleasure of his recovery and the happiness generated by having him return home, pronounced virtually fit. She was of course delighted by this, but privately had to admit that her overriding emotion was one of relief at having the pressure of visits lifted from her overworked shoulders.

She also hoped that his return home might put him in a happier frame of mind. She had sometimes wondered if her visits to the hospital, made with such an effort, had done him any good at all. He had remained morose and, except when complaining, sulkily silent.

Dr North senior simply wanted Jonathan home where he could give him all the help and support that he needed. Nanny Crump wanted to spoil him. 'Feed him some decent food to start with,' she told everyone, as if he'd been on a starvation diet for months.

Mrs Christy was happy that he was coming home, worried about Kate getting overtired and knowing that having him near by would relieve her of some pressure.

Kate knew that Rory and some other members of the staff, although simply pleased that Jonathan was on the mend, were also looking forward to his return to their busy workplace. They didn't know, as she did, that work was the last thing he planned to do, however badly he might be needed. Unless, of course, he had a change of heart once he got home.

The centre had been snowed under by an outbreak of a late summer flu. This had attacked particularly the old, invalids, and children. It had caused havoc with their working schedules, already under strain, and only the determined goodwill and stamina of the whole staff was ensuring that they succeeded in coping with the situation.

Dr Matt North asked for repeat prescriptions to be sent over to him to write up and sign. 'I may be virtually useless on the physical front,' he said to Rory, 'but I've enough strength and gumption to determine if medication is required as per a written or carded request. Anyway, Potty wouldn't let anything slip through that wasn't in order.'

This was true. Mary Potts, of all the staff, rose stoically to the occasion. She worked hours far in excess of those stipulated, and her ability to weed out necessary visits from unnecessary ones was a blessing. In spite of her rather austere façade, she was not the kind of receptionist who took it upon herself to accept or reject a call for help out of hand. Old patients respected her, and new patients soon realised that she was not trying to block their access to a doctor, but establish their need for a visit or attendance at the surgery.

Two days after Jonathan's return home Rory phoned Kate on the intercom and asked her if she could spare the time to have coffee with him in his office. 'Yes,' she said, 'in about twenty minutes when I've finished doing the bloods ready for sending to the lab.'

Rory was immersed in writing up notes and letters when she knocked and entered his office. He lifted his head briefly and gave her a nice smile. 'Won't be a minute,' he said.

Kate set the mugs of coffee that she'd collected from the kitchen down on his desk. She thought how tired he looked. His lean face thinner, the lines down his cheeks more deeply etched. The smattering of grey hairs mingling with the gold above each ear seemed more numerous. With some surprise she realised that it was because his hair was longer. It was also a thick dark bronze on the crown, which made the grey hairs more obvious.

'You need a haircut,' she said involuntarily, and then clapped her hand over her mouth as if to trap the words already uttered.

Rory raised his head and grinned at her. 'Well, nice to think that you've noticed. Would that I had the time.'

'Oh, I am sorry, how rude of me. I do apologise.'

He was still smiling broadly. 'No matter, as I said it's flattering that you've noticed and care about my unshorn locks.' He gave her a steady look from his gold-flecked green eyes. There was a distinct gleam of amusement in them as well as something else which she couldn't fathom.

She smiled rather uncertainly back at him. Because of pressure of work, which ate into their limited leisure time, they hadn't had an opportunity to talk together, except strictly professionally, since the evening meeting. The supper party that her mother had envisaged had not yet taken place. The outbreak of flu had seen to that.

Kate was rather relieved, though why she had reservations about enjoying an innocent meal with Dr North senior, his nephew and her mother she didn't know. It was a gut feeling that the less socialising she did with Rory, the better.

Rory said, his smile now a little taut, 'We've been rather like ships that pass in the night, Kate, haven't we?'

Kate nodded. Was he going to refer to the last occasion that they had spoken with any intimacy? She hoped not. She had managed to put behind her his near kiss and the warm tenderness that he'd displayed later at the meeting. It was only a few days ago, and yet it seemed a lifetime, what with the volume of work that had descended upon them, and Jonathan's return home.

More than ever, she appreciated Rory's professionalism, his dedication to patients and staff under the difficult circumstances that they now found themselves in. He was the rock on which they all depended. His large physical presence in the building was reassuring, and his firm, decided tones a great comfort.

He never seemed to hesitate when making a decision, whether it was Rachel seeking medical advice for a patient, or the young receptionist seeking help on an occasion when both Miss Potts and Kate were absent. Rory was establishing himself as a universal favourite, a doctor *par excellence*. Above all, he wore his authority and caring qualities lightly. No one could accuse him of throwing his weight about. He was ready to listen to as well as give advice.

'A courteous and well-mannered man,' commented Mrs Christy one night when Kate was helping her into bed. 'What a pity his stay in Midchester is only a short one. Even with Jonathan back, Matt will miss him, for according to him they've re-established the rapport that they had before Rory left home years ago.'

Kate had refused to be drawn. Her heart ached for Jonathan who had virtually forecast what would happen once Rory returned. At the same time common sense told her that Rory was not putting on an act. His concern for his uncle, Jonathan and the practice was genuine. He really couldn't help being so charismatic— it was as natural to him as breathing. And yet, with the usual mixture of feelings that seemed to dictate her reactions to him, she felt wary, unsure of herself.

She smiled at Rory, a composed, social smile. 'Yes,'

she confirmed. 'We've been pretty busy, hardly had the opportunity to pass the time of day.' Even to her own ears, her words sounded stilted, contrived; they must sound even more so to him.

If they did, he gave no sign. 'When the pressure is off a bit, and Mike Dolland is back in harness, possibly we can remedy the situation. Go out and have a meal together, perhaps.'

'Perhaps,' Kate said uncertainly.

'But, before that happy situation presents itself,' continued Rory, sounding suddenly brisk, 'I think that we must use our combined efforts to get Jonathan back to work.'

Kate was quite shocked. 'But he's only just come home. You seem to have forgotten that he was injured barely a week ago. He's not fit for work.'

'If he doesn't start soon, Kate, he won't ever be fit for work. His injury was nasty, but it's healing well. You were badly bruised that night, but worked the following day. Jonathan's physical condition isn't any worse than yours was then, or worse than several other people caught up in the bombing. They are back at work. He's fit enough to work, Kate, he really is.'

'No, that's not true.'

'Yes, it is, and I believe that you know it. The psychiatrist at the hospital said as much.' Rory leaned across the desk and put a hand beneath her chin so that she was forced to look at him. 'Didn't Jonathan tell you?' he asked. She wanted to prevaricate, to defend Jonathan, though he'd not even told her that he'd seen a psychiatrist. Her innate honesty and professional integrity made it impossible to answer.

'Ah, you didn't know that he'd seen Dr Wilson!'

Kate shook her head.

'Well, in that case I'm sorry that I jumped the gun and said what I did. Jonathan will want to tell you himself. My apologies. But Kate, as Jonathan's cousin and I hope your friend, not as a doctor, may I suggest that you try to get him to talk about his condition? I don't mean his physical state, but his emotional one.'

'You make it sound as if he's. . .' she hesitated, hating to say what they were both thinking '. . .unstable, or very nearly so, and he's not. He's had a rotten year with his mother dying and his father being ill. It's easy for you to step in now and make all sorts of wild assumptions, but it's just not fair.'

Neither was it fair, she knew, to accuse Rory of making wild assumptions. His remarks were not wild, and deep down she knew that they were not assumptions but basically sound judgements. Even without Dr Wilson's skilled assessment she knew that Jonathan was in need of special help. He had been 'difficult' at times for quite a while; now the shock and the injury he had sustained seemed to have tipped him into a state of melancholy, suspicion and withdrawal.

Rory drew in a sharp breath, then rose from his chair and stood looking out of the clear panes of the window above the frosted lower ones.

He looked very serious, his voice was low and passionate. 'Kate, whatever you may have heard or thought about me, please believe me when I say that I've nothing but goodwill towards Jonathan—if only for my uncle's sake. I believe that only you can persuade him to return to work, and, at this moment in time, work may be his salvation.'

His words and the way that he had uttered them dismayed her. He spoke as if a return to work was Jonathan's last hope. She shivered. 'What do you mean, his salvation?' she asked truculently, angry that her voice trembled.

'Just that, Kate. I'm so sorry, dear girl, but we both have Jonathan's interests at heart. You must have seen changes in him over the past months. Small changes, perhaps. Work, and concern for you and his father, might have enabled him to conceal them to some extent, but I cannot believe that you haven't noticed something.'

Kate remembered Jonathan and his obsession, particularly since his mother's death, with Rory's supposed criminal activities. She recalled his anger when he learned that his father had asked for Rory's help. In fact, he had been quite irrational about the affair, certain that his cousin had suggested coming to help. He had not at first believed, or wanted to believe, that his father had sent for Rory.

And, before that, if she was honest with herself, there had been tiny incidents that had caused her concern. His growing indifference to her mother and Thomas, for instance. That had become more obvious of late. A year ago he would have at least pretended to be interested in their welfare, if only to please Kate, but recently he hadn't bothered to conceal his irritation with the time that she had devoted to them both.

Fortunately, as far as she knew, his withdrawal into his own selfish interests had not affected his dealings with the patients. Those who had been with him since he'd joined the practice several years ago continued to be satisfied with his care. He hadn't, perhaps, inherited that special quality that endeared Dr North senior to his patients, but he was a well-informed and generally caring doctor.

She swallowed her pride and anger and made herself ask calmly, 'Do you think, if Jonathan returns to work, he will improve, get better sooner?'

Rory, still standing at the window, jingled some change in his pocket. He took his time answering, and when he did he spoke slowly and carefully.

'I think, Kate, and I'm not an expert in this field, that Jonathan's *only* chance of improving, at least at present, will be through his work.' He spread his hands in a despairing gesture. 'I can't say more.'

Kate thought about what he had said, and about Jonathan's recent response to her and to others around him. Even before the bombing his reaction to everyday matters had been a little strange at times, his temper uncertain. Work hadn't done much for him then, but if Rory and Dr Wilson both thought that work was his only therapy, then she would do all she could to persuade him to return to the clinic.

'All right,' she said to Rory. 'I'll do my best to get him back on the job.' She managed to raise a smile. 'What a slave-driver he'll think I am.' Secretly she wondered if it would make Jonathan distrust her, believing that she was siding with those he perceived as his enemies. Mentally she gave herself a shake; that she could entertain such a thought meant that she had taken on board the idea that Jonathan was emotionally unstable. This was something that she didn't want to believe.

How long they would have gone on with this discussion was an unknown factor, for suddenly the door was flung open to reveal the white, frightened face of Mary Potts' assistant.

'C-come, come quickly,' she stammered, a sob in her throat.

She stood aside as Rory and Kate moved fast from the room. There was no point in asking her what was wrong. She was clearly too distressed to say.

Once in the corridor they could hear a rumble of sound coming from the waiting-room. When they entered it was to find a small group of people gathered round somebody lying on the floor just inside the entrance doors.

Mary Potts was kneeling beside the prostrate figure of a young girl. Blood was oozing through Mary's fingers, which were locked round the girl's wrists.

A look of immense relief passed over her face as the

doctor and nurse appeared. 'Slashed arteries,' she said, 'but one of them's not too deep.'

Rory knelt down beside the semi-conscious girl. He placed his hands over Mary's. 'Right, I'll take over—now.' Mary slid her hands, crimson with blood, from beneath his, and he continued to apply direct pressure to the gaping wounds.

'I'll fetch pads,' Kate said to Rory, and to Linda, who, though white and obviously terrified, was standing her ground, 'Take Miss Potts through to wash her hands, and make a big pot of tea.' Kate was moving fast towards the clinic-room as she spoke. She turned to the group of patients standing transfixed about Rory and the girl. 'Please go and sit down; we'll get things sorted out as soon as possible.'

She saw that among the group was a retired nurse, a bright lady and reasonably fit. 'Mrs Bates, will you fetch a wheelchair? There are some at the end of the corridor.'

'Right, Sister, will do.'

Kate collected pads and bandages and in seconds was back kneeling beside Rory. Most of the patients had moved away, though only a couple had sat down—the rest were standing in an uneasy group, murmuring quietly. Mrs Bates returned with the chair. Kate thanked her and suggested that she might go and see if Linda and Miss Potts were all right. 'Perhaps you can help speed up the tea-making and dish some out to everyone,' she said, managing to flash her a smile as she secured a pad over one wrist of the girl on the floor.

Mrs Bates, with a reassuring nod, disappeared through the door to the corridor. Kate and Rory tried to fix a pad on to the other wrist but blood was gushing from the partially severed radial artery. 'Pull the edges together and keep on with direct pressure,' muttered Rory as he lifted the inert form on to the wheelchair and hastened towards the clinic-room. 'We'll want an ambulance and I want clamps, silk or gut for ligaturing, adrenalin and forceps,' he said.

Using both hands, and easing together the jagged flesh of the untidy cuts, Kate tried to stem the flow of blood spurting from the radial artery. She applied direct pressure with a pad and rolled up bandages and raised the girl's arm as they wheeled her from the waiting-room. Even then, in the middle of an emergency, she noticed how quickly Rory donned the manners of a consultant, issuing a stream of orders, certain that he would be obeyed.

Mary Potts, looking deathly pale but otherwise as usual, was drying her hands at the sink as they entered the clinic-room.

'Shall I phone for an ambulance?' she asked.

'Please,' replied Kate. 'Thanks for keeping her ticking over.' She indicated the prone patient now lying on the examination couch and gave the receptionist a smile.

Rory briefly raised his head and smiled at her too. 'Well done, Potty,' he said, and the deliberate use of his uncle's affectionate nickname for her obviously did wonders for her morale.

'I'll go and sort things out,' she replied, and left for the reception area.

The next ten minutes were a race against time. Rory took over pressurising the girl's wrist while Kate collected the items that he had requested. They worked quietly together, both knowing exactly what to do as Rory attempted to ligature off the damaged ends of the artery. Even with Kate applying pressure and swabbing with or dripping adrenalin on to the wound, there was an excessive flow of blood. But Rory managed to first clamp and then tie off the ends of the severed artery. He pulled the skin together and Kate clipped it with skin suture to hold pro tem before covering the whole area with an oxydised cellulose sterile pad and bandaging it into position.

Meanwhile Rory was slightly loosening the pad on the other wrist, without disturbing the dressing. The blood here had diminished to a trickle. He placed another pad over the original and secured it in position. 'Nothing much more we can do now, Kate,' he said, examining the pupils of the girl's eyes and taking her temporal pulse, 'except keep her warm and as comfortable as possible, and elevate the foot of the couch. I daren't give her a stimulant of any sort lest it increase her blood-pressure too much and puts unacceptable strain on these.' He indicated the padded wrists. 'But I'd like to have an idea of her pressure. I'll have a listen; it might tell me something.'

Kate nodded; she had placed a blanket over the girl to keep her warm and to some extent counteract the shock caused by blood loss. There was a limit to what they could do, but checking the blood-pressure would give Rory some idea as to what lengths he might need to go if the pressure dropped alarmingly. He wouldn't be able to use the sphygmo and ordinary blood-pressure equipment; it would be dangerous. He would have to rely on his hearing, the infinitesimal changes of volume through his ears, and on instinct.

She handed him a stethoscope. 'Just depress very gently above the brachial artery on the less damaged arm,' he instructed Kate. 'And I'll hear what I can.' He placed the head of his stethoscope over the crease in the elbow where the large blood-vessel, the brachial artery, passed near the surface. 'I don't want to muck up the flow too much—might start the bleeding off again.' He listened carefully through the stethoscope to judge at what point the volume of blood cut out and then resumed as Kate slowly released her pressure on the arm. It would give him a rough idea of what was happening.

They both knew that he was simply trying to do something, anything to help the patient while waiting for the ambulance to arrive. The only hopeful information he might get was that there had been a rise in blood-pressure following their treatment to reduce haemorrhage. If the girl's blood-pressure had fallen to a very low level Rory might have to make a difficult choice without the back-up of a hospital team, medication and equipment.

Would he decide to give a stimulant of some sort as being the lesser of two evils, at the risk of causing further haemorrhage? What the girl really needed was blood, fluids and plasma fast to replace the loss.

At that moment the intermittent howl of the ambulance siren penetrated the walls of the centre.

'Thank God,' said Rory fervently.

The ambulance men had gone, taking with them their pathetic passenger. She had started to rouse as they were putting her in the ambulance. 'What's your name, love?' asked one of the men.

'Karen,' whispered the ghost-white girl. 'Karen Strong.'

'OK. Karen, we'll take care of you till we get you to the hospital. Where do you live?'

'London,' she murmured. 'I live in London.' And then she slipped again into unconsciousness.

Several of the patients who had been in the reception area when she'd arrived had followed the men out to the ambulance. There was nothing anyone could do about it. They were determined to see her installed in the vehicle.

One of them, overhearing what the girl had said, pulled Kate aside. 'She don't live in London,' she said. 'Leastways, it's not her proper home. Her people live just outside the town, the other side of the river. They keep a guest-house or something.'

'Right, Mrs Langley,' said Kate, heaving a sigh of relief. 'That's just the sort of thing that we want to know. Miss Potts will try to get in touch with her parents.'

Mrs Langley swelled visibly, pleased with the effect that her words had had on the sister in charge of the centre. Kate bit back the question that was waiting to be asked, silently wondering why the silly woman hadn't divulged her information earlier.

Rory and Kate stood outside the centre for a few minutes after the ambulance had left, watching it disappear down the road. They needed a breather. Most of the patients who had been on the premises returned to the reception-room. Some had only come to collect medicine, but no way were they going to miss any of the post-emergency excitement.

'Poor kid, she must have been desperate,' Rory said softly. 'Do you know who she is?'

'No, I don't think she's on our list, but another patient knows something about her. Her people live across the river.'

'I wonder why she chose to do what she did here?' said Rory, staring down at the ground by his feet. 'You realise that she'd only just cut herself, don't you?'

'Yes, and with something jagged and not too clean.'

For a brief moment they stared at each other. Then in unison said, 'Bottle bank.' The bottle bank was situated on a piece of waste ground behind the parade of shops next to the centre's car park.

Rory and Kate followed the trail of blood leading to the thin wire fence that formed the boundary. Beside the bottle container lay a shattered bottle, and, beside the broken glass, a pool of blood. This was obviously the spot where Karen Strong had slashed her wrists.

Kate felt herself trembling. Tears filled her eyes and she turned away from Rory so that he should not see them. 'How terribly, terribly sad,' she said in a wobbly voice.

'Yes,' confirmed Rory. 'How very sad, poor child. I wonder why?' He put out a hand and touched Kate's arm. 'Come on, my dear, we've still work to do.' He guided her back to the centre.

They asked everyone present in the waiting-room if they had seen anything that might help them solve the mystery of the young girl. Had anyone been with her when she'd entered? Nobody had seen anyone. Had she said anything? No, she had staggered in through the doors and collapsed, bleeding profusely. Everyone remarked on the blood.

'I must get this cleared up,' said Kate, noticing for the first time the splashes and smears of blood just inside the door.

'Isn't there someone who can do this for you?' asked Rory.

'No, Dot Harrison isn't due in till later, none of the other nurses will be back till after lunch, and young Linda isn't up to it. I don't mind, really. It won't be the first time I've cleared up a spot of blood.' She smiled at him and went off to collect a rubber apron, gloves and a bucket of hot water.

When she came back Rory was still there in the waiting-room talking to Mary Potts, who was still trying to get hold of the Strongs.

'I'll help,' he said, and took the brush from her. 'I'll scrub, you mop.'

She wanted to protest, but could see that he was determined. 'If you insist,' she replied, returning his smile.

'Oh, I do,' he said, and started scrubbing.

The rest of the day passed uneventfully. Mary Potts eventually succeeded in contacting the Strongs. They were devastated to learn what had happened to their daughter. Apparently they'd had a disagreement about her wanting to go to London and live with a friend, and had no idea that she was so upset.

Driving home just after six o'clock, Kate thought about what Rory and she had been discussing when the emergency arose. Well, she would tackle Jonathan tonight about starting work. Somehow, seeing that young girl who had slashed her wrists, who was so desperate, gave her confidence. It seemed quite clear now that Jonathan should try to work again, as soon as possible.

To Kate's surprise, Jonathan was quite co-operative when she saw him that evening. 'You're right, Kate, as usual,' he said. 'I should get back into harness again.' He seemed, for the first time since the bombing, to be normal and loving towards her. Her heart rejoiced; perhaps the shock had triggered off a new era, perhaps they would get back on to the gentle, loving wavelength that they had enjoyed months ago.

She found it easy to dismiss the increasingly strange behaviour that he had exhibited since his mother died, and especially since his injury over the last week or so. It was as if those uncomfortable visits to the hospital, and his withdrawal, had never happened. In fact, his enthusiastic suggestion that he would be in the surgery for eight-thirty in the morning was worrying.

'Jonathan, darling, don't do that, please. You're on the mend but not yet a hundred per cent. Why don't you come in at eleven and supervise the pre-natal clinic? The new "nearly mums" will be delighted to see you.'

'Really? Are you sure that they wouldn't rather have my esteemed cousin, Sir Perfect Rowland?'

Oh, no, thought Kate, don't spoil it. Aloud she said, 'What all our regular patients need is continuity, Jonathan. True, they might want your dad, but failing him you'll do very nicely, thank you.' She prayed that she'd struck the right note, and apparently she had. Being compared to his father bolstered him no end.

'In that case, Sister, expect me to report for duty at eleven on the dot.'

Kate kissed him lovingly. 'Your word is my command, Doctor,' she said with a gentle chuckle.

She drove home feeling happier and more at ease with the world than she had for a long time. Jonathan was almost back to normal, Mike Dolland would be home from the Pyrenees next week, and old Dr North was making good progress following his heart attack.

What more could she want? she thought happily, as she made ready for bed. Nothing, she told herself as she began to fall asleep. Nothing? Something niggled in her mind. There was a flaw somewhere, but she could not identify what it was that was marring her total contentment. It was with some difficulty that she squashed these fears before falling into a deep, sound sleep.

CHAPTER SEVEN

DURING the following week Jonathan went into the centre every day and took over several clinics. It was an ideal way for him to get back to full-time work as clinics more or less ran on time, ensuring that he could take rest periods regularly. He seemed well, but occasionally complained of headaches.

'Perhaps you should see someone about these headaches,' Kate suggested one day. 'After all, you did have a head injury.'

'Facial,' replied Jonathan tersely. 'And who would you suggest that I consult—my revered cousin?'

Kate ignored that childish remark. She would have liked to suggest Dr Wilson, the psychiatrist, but since Jonathan had never mentioned him to her she couldn't very well throw his name into the discussion.

Kate found Jonathan's continuing animosity towards Rory rather trying. His cousin was bending over backwards to make sure that Jonathan was accorded the respect due to the role of chief in the practice.

It wasn't easy for him, as most of the staff, and many of the patients, seemed to look upon him as the senior member of the medical staff. Of course, he was, if one considered qualifications and status. Rory was the undisputed leader of the local medical fraternity. He was a consultant paediatrician, and, though it hadn't been verified, it was rumoured that he would soon be appointed one of the youngest professors in his field when he took over a new unit in a teaching hospital the following year.

Kate was working in her office and as usual immersed in paperwork at the end of a long day on duty when

Mike Dolland appeared. He had just arrived back from his holiday and heard of the bombing and the sub-sequent problems it had produced at the centre. He wasn't due back on duty until the day after tomorrow, but when he heard the news he insisted on coming back the following day.

'Why ever didn't you try to reach me?' he asked. 'I left poste restante addresses for use in an emergency.'

'Well, it wouldn't have been easy, contacting some remote village high in the Pyrenees, but I would have done if Rowland North hadn't arrived to help out.'

Mike whistled through his teeth. '*The* Rowland North?' he asked. 'He of infamous memory, who left the old man high and dry aeons ago?'

'If you mean Dr Matt North's nephew,' replied Kate primly, 'yes, he came to our rescue. Dr North sent for him when your locum went sick.'

'Well, I bet that didn't go down too well in some quarters. Jonathan has never made any secret about hating his guts.'

Normally, Kate rather liked Mike Dolland. He was cheerful, happily married with two teenage children whom he obviously adored, and could be relied upon to keep his cool under most circumstances. Now, looking at him, a healthy leather-brown from his walk in the high Alps, she could have strangled him.

He was untouched by all that had happened over the last couple of weeks. It wasn't his fault, but he had simply been absent when something of enormous importance had occurred in Midchester, and yet he had the gall to make jokes about the situation.

As if homing in on her unspoken criticism, Mike said, with some humility, 'Sorry, that was out of order. Family matters, and you are almost North family. I apologise.'

His apology mended the moment. 'It's all right,' Kate replied. 'I suppose your reaction is what one might expect.' She smiled at him. 'Anyway, it's nice of you to call in so promptly.'

There was a knock at her door, and to her invitation to come in Rory entered. 'Oh, sorry, am I interrupting?' he asked.

'No, not at all, come and meet Mike Dolland, of whom you have heard much, but seen not at all,' replied Kate. He stepped further into the room, and Kate was conscious of how pleased she was to see him. It was as if he, Rory had been away, not Mike, and she suddenly knew that in a sense he had. He'd been avoiding her since Jonathan had returned to work.

With a catch in her breath, which she turned into an acceptable cough as Rory gave her an enigmatic look, she introduced the two men.

They shook hands, and Kate sensed at once that they liked each other.

'Whereabouts did you wander in the mountains?' asked Rory in a voice that Kate fancied was deeper than usual.

'All over the place, following in the footsteps of J. B. Morton in the twenties.'

'Didn't he write something about fleas in the Pyrenees?'

'Yes, and much more besides—a great humorist. You must come and have supper with us some time, and be bored by our holiday snaps, and a kilometre by kilometre description of our journey. I'll have a word with Bella—my wife,' he explained.

'I should like that.'

Kate intervened. 'Mike has offered to come on duty tomorrow instead of the next day,' she said. 'Perhaps you'd like to sort out some duties between you?'

'I think that we should see what Jonathan thinks,' said Rory. 'Is he still here?' As he asked the totally innocent question his eyes met Kate's. For a moment a stillness descended on the room as she and Rory stared at each other.

'No, he left about half an hour ago at the end of his clinic,' she heard herself answer in a cool little voice.

Rory looked away from her and towards Mike. 'Come along to Uncle Matt's office,' he invited him, 'and we'll phone Jonathan.'

After they had gone Kate sat at her desk, staring into space. Had she imagined the intense look that Rory had focused on her? Had she responded in like manner, with her eyes full of the same intangible emotion that she'd read in his? It was ridiculous— there had been a third person in the room, nice, sensible Mike. Nothing so earth-shattering could have happened without his being aware of it. Or could it? Could so much have been said, and yet not said, in so small a fraction of time that Mike hadn't even noticed the stillness, the utter quiet that had filled her office?

She tried to concentrate on her work, but for once professional training and discipline failed to come to her aid. She was tormented by the memory of Rory's eyes boring into hers. Other incidents came to mind that had occurred over the last few days. Incidents that had registered on her subconscious without her realising it.

Rory had been considerate and attentive at the second self-help meeting, which Jonathan had reluctantly agreed to attend. However, it was to do much for his morale. Everyone had been quick to welcome him back as their doctor and as someone who had experienced the full horror of injury as a result of the bombing. And, once Jonathan was fully occupied with other people, Rory had seldom left her side.

Their conversation had been quite innocent, mostly professional, concerned with the reason for the meeting, and yet. . . He had brushed against her, leaning across to greet somebody, and his touch had made her tremble. 'Cold?' he'd asked solicitously, eyes gleaming as they had this evening with a mixture of emotion. They had both known that to be cold was impossible in the warm room.

Kate had kept up the pretence that her reaction to him had a more mundane cause. 'Someone walking over my grave,' she said, managing a tremulous smile.

'Ah,' he replied, 'is that what it was?'

Kate had nodded, not trusting herself to speak. Later she'd decided that the sensation of floating and being detached from her surroundings had existed only in her imagination. Except that, as she and Jonathan were leaving, Rory had said, in the most ordinary fashion, but with his eyes lingering on her, 'A successful evening, I think, don't you?'

Jonathan, still enjoying the euphoria of being the man of the moment, was for once in a friendly frame of mind towards his cousin. He said cheerfully, 'Very. It was a splendid idea of yours, Rory, these meetings.'

A lesser man, thought Kate, would have shown his surprise at this unexpected compliment, but Rory simply breathed in rather sharply and replied evenly, 'Well, thank you, Jonathan. Nice of you to say so.'

Rory absented himself from the third meeting, making it clear that Jonathan was in charge. 'I'm on call,' he said to Kate, 'and have a hell of a lot of reading to catch up with. Anyway, it's much more appropriate that Jonathan puts in an appearance; he was, after all, involved.'

Kate had been surprised at her feeling of disappointment that he wouldn't be at the meeting. She was unable to explain to herself why she regretted his absence then, and yet made a point of avoiding him when she knew that she might bump into him at her home or at his Uncle Matt's.

This revelation brought her up short. Until now, she hadn't examined or even considered her reactions to

Rory or his presence anywhere. Why did he now figure so prominently in her thoughts? Why did she look forward to enjoying his company on the one hand, and avoid it on the other? Was part of her interest in him born out of her sense of fair play, because Jonathan persisted in making him out to be a charlatan?

Wearily she wondered what it was that Rory had wanted to see her about. Surely it couldn't have been important? She had seen very little of him in the past week, except during working hours or at the second special meeting. It did look as if he was avoiding her. It wasn't difficult to guess that her closeness to Jonathan, and his continuing dislike of Rory, had something to do with it. So what had he wanted with her this evening that only the unexpected arrival of Mike Dolland had prevented him divulging? Was it a professional matter, or a personal one?

If, Kate wondered, she had been less involved with Jonathan, would Rory and she have become more friendly? Perhaps if they had met under other circumstances, they would. . . Abruptly she put a stop to these thoughts. They were ridiculous and dangerous.

She and Jonathan had had what amounted to an understanding, for years. Only the bomb that night had stopped him asking her to marry him. Before that, his mother had been something of an obstacle to his declaring himself, though he had never admitted this. And, of course, there was always her mother and Thomas. Jonathan found it hard to understand her devotion to them. But any problems could, and would, be overcome. Jonathan's health would continue to improve and they would get married as planned. To hell with the charismatic Rory North!

With Jonathan and Mike back, and the flu mini-demic subsiding, life had become less hectic, and everyone was able to take some time off.

Rory had called in a couple of times at Bathurst, so Mrs Christy had told Kate. 'He brought Matt over yesterday, and collected Thomas from school to save Dora a trip. Have you noticed that she's been a bit off colour?'

Kate hadn't noticed, and was full of compunction for not having done so. She also realised, with some guilt, that, because Thomas had been dressing and undressing himself without argument recently, she had missed out on tales of Rory's visits.

Kate spent most of her evenings with Jonathan, often in his flat. Sometimes they would drive around the lovely autumn-tinted countryside drenched in early evening sunshine. They would stop for a meal or a drink, and drive back under the golden light of a huge harvest moon.

Jonathan's moods were erratic. He was alternately cool and friendly, or impatiently amorous, when his kisses and caresses were savage and demanding rather than loving. But on the whole he was more amiable, less given to bouts of anger than over recent months.

Kate had to be satisfied with this. She would have liked to stay at home some evenings, either with her mother and Thomas, or with old Dr North, but Jonathan would have none of it.

'Dad's got his wonderful Rory,' he said on one occasion, with a return to his old bitterness. 'And your mother and Thomas take up enough of your time as it is. Surely they don't begrudge me a little of your company?'

Tentatively Kate said, 'I just thought how nice it would be if we all had an evening together for once.'

'Playing happy families, you mean,' replied Jonathan, half joking, half sarcastic.

'Why not?' Kate answered cheerfully, determined not to take offence and remembering her mother's suggestion about inviting the North men for a meal. At the time she had meant Matt and Rory, but she would be happy to have Jonathan. 'Mother would love to have a nice little supper party to celebrate your safe return home. She was very concerned about you when you were in hospital.'

'Really?'

'Yes, really,' said Kate sharply.

Jonathan could see that she was angry. 'Sorry, darling,' he said apologetically, kissing her softly on her cheek. 'I'm just greedy to have you to myself, I suppose; but you're quite right, we should have a get-together. You fix it and I'll be on my best behaviour.'

The supper party was fixed for a week later. It had turned into a much larger affair than originally planned. Mrs Christy and Dora had really gone to town and decided to invite all the practice doctors, and, in Mike's case, his wife Bella, too. They'd also asked Mary Potts, as senior receptionist and an old friend.

Apparently, Rachel Lyons, true to the shyness that Rory had pointed out, had at first refused the invitation, until he, at Mrs Christy's behest, had persuaded her to come.

'But I shall be on call,' she had protested to Kate's mother.

'My dear, I don't know that I ever gave a party when at least one of my guests wasn't on call,' she replied cheerfully. 'The penalty of being married to a GP, and now with a daughter who is virtually wedded to the health centre—an uninterrupted meal is a luxury.'

'Well, as long as you understand if I have to leave suddenly.'

'My dear girl, of course I'll understand; just come and enjoy yourself.'

* * *

On the morning of the supper party Kate arrived at the centre early, determined to get through some of the mound of paperwork before what she considered the real day's work began. For once, she promised herself, she would get off duty on time to help her mother and Dora with the chores.

To her surprise, she found that the outer double locks of the doors were undone; only the ordinary lock was functioning. Somebody, possibly the doctor on night calls, was inside the building. All the doctors, as well as Mary Potts and herself, had keys, and with the crisis of staff shortages over it was unlikely to be Mary already on duty.

She called, 'Hello,' as she let herself in, and Rory at once appeared in the opening leading from the corridor into the waiting-room.

'Hi,' he said, sounding infinitely weary. 'You're early.' He'd obviously not had time to shave, for, as she'd noticed on another occasion, his chin was thick with dark bristles.

For a moment, Kate thought that her heart had stopped, so breathless did she find herself at the unexpected encounter. She pulled herself together.

'Lots to do,' she explained briefly.

He still stood four-square in the opening to the corridor. 'Of course—party tonight. Want to help your mother and Dora.' He passed a hand over his thick thatch of hair. 'Better go home and have a wash and brush-up.'

'Night call?' asked Kate.

'Would you believe, three?' he said with a lop-sided grin. 'I don't know how these GPs manage. They're bloody marvellous!'

'You might spread that around a bit when you get back to the dizzy heights of the hospital consultants' world,' Kate said with a smile. 'GPs are still considered the lowliest of the medical profession, aren't they?'

'Yes—quite erroneously, of course.'

Kate had moved forward so that she was standing just in front of him. He drew her like a magnet. She longed to put out a hand and touch his unshaven cheek. The thought made her gasp with surprise.

He took a step towards her and grasped her arms. 'Kate, are you all right?'

She was furious with herself. She shrugged off his hands. 'Of course I am,' she said angrily. 'Look, please let me pass. I want to get on.'

He lifted his hands from her arms. 'Oh, Kate,' he said thickly in a muffled voice.

Her heart lurched. 'Rory,' she breathed uncertainly.

'Kate?' There was a questioning, elated lilt to his voice, and then his arms were around her and his stubbly chin was scraping against her cheek. 'Kate, Kate,' he repeated, and then his lips found hers, and his tongue probed and prodded until her lips opened under the onslaught and she returned his kisses with a warmth and sensuousness that matched his own.

They stood wrapped together in each other's arms for an unknown period of time, exchanging kiss for kiss on a rising tide of euphoria. At some point, Rory drew Kate back into his office and he sat down on his desk chair with her still in his arms. They exchanged words and half-broken sentences of endearments between their rough and fierce kisses. Neither was really aware of what was said, or where they were.

It was Kate who abruptly drew away from Rory, sensing that someone had come into the building.

Mary Potts called out, 'It's only me.' Kate heard the familiar sounds of Mary walking through to the staff cloakroom and hanging up her coat before moving in to the reception office.

Rory and Kate stood facing each other in his room, just a foot or so apart. His sea-green eyes were at once dark yet glowing with the gold flecks that lit them from time to time. His lips, usually rather thin, though well marked, were red and full because Kate had returned his passionate kisses in kind. Her own felt sore, thickened. She stared at him, astonished. Had they given way to such an explosion of emotion and passion? It was hard to believe possible in the clinical surroundings of the health centre.

Somehow they separated, he going through the reception area and calling to Miss Potts that he would be back in time for surgery, and she to her office.

Kate put in an appearance a short time after Rory had left. 'I'm trying to get on with some paperwork before the rush begins,' she explained to an unsurprised Mary Potts.

'I expect you want to get off early,' said Mary indulgently. 'To help your mother and Dora with the preparations for this evening. I'm sure that we're all looking forward to the party.'

Kate agreed. She gave herself a good talking to on returning to her office, and took two paracetamols with a cup of coffee.

The morning was very busy. Mike, with the enthusiasm of someone who had recently been on holiday, sent her a stream of patients for blood samples and sputum and urine tests. He also wanted an ECG done on an elderly lady, a new patient to the practice, who was showing signs of respiratory and circulatory problems.

He phoned Kate on the intercom. 'Can you do this immediately?' he asked. 'I'm rather bothered about this lady.'

'Of course, at once,' replied Kate.

She did the ECG, and phoned him back with the report from her office while the patient was getting dressed in the clinic-room. 'I'll bring along the readout if you're free,' she said, 'but you're right to be bothered. Mrs Green is in big trouble; there is evidence of a myocardial infarction and associated irregularities.'

Mike groaned. 'Thanks, Kate, that's what I suspected. Any idea what the position is *re* admissions to St Just's, or the Cottage Hospital?'

'Both full, as far as I know, except for emergencies. You might get Mrs Green in under that category, if that's what you were thinking. It's worth a try. Would you like me to sus them out while you have a word with the patient?'

'Bless you, if you would. Are you sure that you've got time?'

Kate assured him that she had. More than anything she wanted to keep busy in an effort to blot out what had happened between her and Rory that morning. She didn't even feel equal to trying to think out the implications of their mutual outburst of emotion.

Thank goodness she hadn't seen Jonathan. He'd left to do his rounds before she was free of patients, so she had been spared any embarrassment in a confrontation with him. Whether he would have guessed that she was on edge, or, if he had, remotely suspected the reason for it, she didn't know, but she would have felt unable to deal with him.

Rory too had left on his rounds without her seeing him during the course of the morning. She felt both relieved and deprived by his absence, a curious state of emotion that remained with her for the rest of the day. Fortunately, Jonathan, whom she still dreaded meeting, phoned late morning to say that he would go straight to the surgery held at a nearby village that afternoon, after having lunch at home.

'So I'll see you this evening, Kate, at your mother's supper party, which seems to have turned into quite an elaborate affair.'

'It's only our close friends,' said Kate defensively. 'It's a long time since we had a get-together off duty. I'm sure that you'll enjoy it once we get started.'

'Well, I can put up with most of them, I suppose, and tolerate the presence of my illustrious cousin for a few hours. Anyway, it doesn't matter—he'll be returning to the flesh-pots of Harley Street before long.'

Kate was shocked into silence. Was Jonathan speaking from knowledge of Rory's movements, or was it wishful thinking on his part? Or, and the thought made her inwardly catch her breath, did he know something about what had happened that morning between her and Rory and was punishing her for her infidelity?

She was so quiet that Jonathan asked her if she was still there. 'Yes, of course I am,' she managed to say firmly. To placate him further, she asked, 'How were your rounds today—I bet your patients were pleased to see you back?'

'Oh, they're all right,' he said indifferently. 'The old seem older, and the difficult ones even more difficult. I think they've saved up all their grumbles for me.'

Kate sought frantically for the right words. 'They probably have—they're used to you, Jonathan, especially the older patients; they don't like change.'

'Probably,' he said in a still complaining voice, though he sounded somewhat mollified. 'See you tonight, then.'

Kate had brought sandwiches for lunch so that she could eat and work at the same time in order to get away sharp that evening. The centre was closed from one till two, and for once was quite empty. Everyone who was not going home had gathered in the pub opposite for a snack.

She sat in her office nibbling in a half-hearted fashion at her food, while trying to concentrate on lab forms and duty rosters. The desire to see Rory was overwhelming, and yet she prayed that he wouldn't return to find her alone. When she heard the front doors being unlocked and heard him call out, she took herself off to the cloakroom, and locked the door.

With a tremendous effort, she stopped herself rushing out and into his arms when he called, 'Kate, are you there?' She heard him go through to her office and the treatment-room, and swear softly when he didn't find her. He obviously didn't suspect that she might be hiding from him. Presently he left the building and she heard him double-locking the doors behind him. With luck, she wouldn't have to face him until tonight at the party.

He was taking the afternoon off. A much needed and overdue break which he so deserved, so she would be safe from a chance encounter with him for several hours. But her mixture of emotions remained with her. She both wanted to see him, and at the same time shied away from the inevitable meeting that night.

She had been all in favour of the party and the opportunity that it provided for Jonathan to start socialising again—now she was dreading it. She didn't trust her reactions to Rory in front of Jonathan, whose antipathy to his cousin made him super-sensitive to everything connected with him.

How was she going to disguise her feelings for the man whom Jonathan so disliked and distrusted? And for how long could she keep up the charade of loving one man while knowing that her heart belonged to another?

She was shocked at the way her thoughts were taking her. What she was saying was that she was in love with Rory North—in love—like some romantic heroine in a cheap novelette? Ridiculous! How could she be? They had only known each other for a few weeks—she hadn't even *liked* him when they'd first met.

What had he done, until today, to show the depth of his feelings? There had been a few moments, tender moments, they seemed on reflection, when he had shown he cared more than a little. . .and she had chosen to deny them. . .because of Jonathan?

With a great effort she pulled herself together. She went through to the cloakroom, washed her face, put on a little make-up and combed her hair before returning to her office.

What a bloody mess life had suddenly become, she thought, and tonight at the party she would have to face both men.

CHAPTER EIGHT

IN FACT, the party didn't turn out to be the ordeal that Kate had expected.

The moment of truth, she said to herself as she joined her mother and Dora to welcome the guests.

She was wearing a full crushed-velvet skirt the colour of ripe loganberries, topped with a demure white high-necked cotton blouse. She felt, and knew, that she looked good, in a cool, rather remote fashion. Her favourite floral perfume, lavishly splashed on, clung about her like the sharp scent of young tea-roses in their first bloom.

A few minutes after she had come downstairs, Jonathan arrived with his father, always a stickler for punctuality. Kate went to let them in through the wide hall and along the narrow passage leading to the Victorian conservatory where the buffet supper had been laid out.

'Enchanting,' said Dr North, admiring the soft lamp-light reflected in the myriad panes and the soaring curved glass roof. 'I'd forgotten how attractive this could be.' He looked round at the potted plants and hanging baskets with approval. Before he sat down, he bowed slightly over their hands—Maddy's, Dora's and Kate's—and repeated, 'Enchanting,' as he did so. Kate fancied that he held her mother's hand a little longer and inclined his head rather lower when greeting her. She could see that her mother was conscious of this too, and was blushing faintly.

What a pretty woman Ma is, she thought.

Jonathan simply said, though very nicely, 'Every-thing looks great,' and, with an attempt at gallantry, added, 'and if I may say so, so do you ladies.' This pleased Mrs Christy and Dora, who were aware that he was making an effort to be especially pleasant.

He gave Kate a long, appreciative look, arching his eyebrows high over his blue eyes, which tonight were bright and unclouded.

'Wow, you look stunning!' he murmured as she offered a cheek to be kissed.

This carefree, casual compliment set the seal upon the evening for Kate. Jonathan's obvious normality cheered her enormously. Her feelings for Rory, and the passion of the morning meeting, seemed less immediately threatening in the face of Jonathan's spontaneous and uncomplicated words. She realised that she didn't have to make decisions for a bit. Time would help resolve her problems. Jonathan would continue to improve and be less vulnerable for a start. It was in a state of mild euphoria that she faced the rest of the evening, and the inevitable meeting with Rory.

Old Dr North, noticing Thomas, who'd been allowed to stay up to greet the guests as a special treat, asked, 'Is this young man in charge of the drinks?'

Thomas, who rather liked the old doctor, said shyly, 'Gran says that I can help to give out glasses and these.' He thrust a dish of peanuts at Dr North.

'Ah, just what I want to go with a wee dram,' said the doctor, who occasionally remembered his far-distant Scottish ancestry. He took a handful of nuts and bent his head towards Thomas. 'Do you think that Jonathan might pour drinks for the ladies, and one for you and me?' he asked. 'You can hand them round.'

Thomas bounced up and down with excitement and rushed over to Jonathan. 'Will you?' he asked. 'Will you pour out the drinks? I'll take them round, and Dr North wants a wee dram. If we've got that,' he said, eyeing the bottles anxiously, 'and I want a Coke, please.'

For one moment Kate thought that Jonathan was going to brush the boy aside, as he so often did. But his happy mood held and he bent down and whispered in Thomas's ear. 'You go and find out what the ladies want, and I'll sort out the wee dram.'

The party, having got off to a good start, continued in the same vein. When Rory arrived he was escorting Rachel—a fact that seemed to please Jonathan no end.

'Well, well, well,' he breathed in Kate's ear. 'Is that the way that the land lies?'

Kate was torn between relief that Jonathan was reassured by the two arriving together and a totally unexpected attack of jealousy at seeing them arm in arm. She knew that it was ridiculous, and that Rory's hand beneath Rachel's elbow was merely that of a courteous escort. She successfully regained her composure, and gave them a warm welcome.

Rory was his usual calm self and returned her greeting cheerfully as he gently propelled his shy companion into the room. Somehow he managed to hand her over into Jonathan's care, so that for a moment he and Kate were left, in the most natural fashion, alone.

He looked handsome and rather aloof as he stood just inside the conservatory, his wide shoulders propped against the door frame. It seemed impossible, a dream almost, that he had held her so passionately in his arms that morning.

His sea-green eyes glinted. 'Your mother's a great gardener,' he said, indicating the masses of blooms standing on the slatted benches. 'I've seen them in daylight, of course, but I believe they look even more magnificent in lamplight.'

He turned away from the plants and eyed Kate, scanning her from top to toe. Jonathan was busy talking to Rachel and plying her with food and drink. The gold flecks in his eyes gleamed brighter. 'You look beautiful,' he murmured, 'and your scent is delightful.' His smile sent the blood rushing to her cheeks and her heart pounding.

She said primly, in an effort to hide her reaction, 'You'd better come and say hello to everyone, and grab something to eat.' With difficulty she made herself move away from him, and somehow found the courage to give him a dazzling smile.

'Wonderful,' he said softly, and stepped forward to greet her mother and the other guests. Thomas positively flung himself at Rory, confirming what Mrs Christy had said about him understanding the boy.

Jonathan said sharply, 'Shouldn't Thomas be in bed by now?' A reminder that his equanimity was still fragile.

'It's Friday,' said Kate. 'No school tomorrow; we let him stay up a bit later.' She smiled. 'Don't you think it's lovely to see him so happy?'

'Hmm, yes, yes, of course.' He didn't sound too sure, but, remembering how nice he had been at the start of the evening, Kate felt that she couldn't complain.

Thomas, encouraged by Rory, agreed to go to bed eventually. Kate went up with him to tuck him in. He looked angelic in his striped pyjamas. Kate gave him a kiss and a hug. 'Goodnight, love,' she said, 'sleep tight.'

'I like Rory,' remarked Thomas. 'Do you like Rory, Kate?'

'Yes,' replied Kate honestly. 'I like Rory.'

'That's good,' said Thomas, half asleep. 'I'm glad.'

Kate kissed him again on the forehead, and went downstairs. She found to her surprise that she was able to carry on perfectly normal conversations with other people in spite of being constantly aware of Rory's presence.

Occasionally she caught his eye, and was reminded of the line from the song, something about 'across a crowded room'. And I'd like to fly to his side, and never let him go, she paraphrased silently. Such fanciful thoughts brought on an attack of the giggles, which she struggled to suppress. Kate wondered what Bella Dolland, to whom she was talking, would think if she knew what was going through her mind. Fortunately, Bella was so intent on extolling the virtues of the crusty bread and goat's cheese that they'd eaten on top of a Pyrenean mountain that she didn't notice Kate's barely controlled explosion of mirth.

The heavily laden buffet table was beginning to look like a battlefield, when the phone went.

'For whom the bell tolls,' shouted the medical fraternity. 'It tolls for thee, Rachel.'

It did indeed, and Rachel, who, once she had got over her shyness, had begun to enjoy herself, left reluctantly.

'I'll go with you,' said Rory, when he learned the name of the patient who had rung in. 'He's one of mine, and a bit of a problem.' He turned to Mrs Christy. 'I'm sure you understand. Thank you for a lovely party, it's been great.'

Rachel said her goodbyes and thanked her hostess.

'You must come again, and soon,' said Mrs Christy.

'Please,' replied Rachel. 'I should like that very much.'

Kate felt hollow after Rory had gone, though she concealed this successfully and continued to respond to Jonathan's good humour. I must hold on for a bit, she told herself, and in time everything will become clear.

Just before the party wound up, Mike Dolland drifted across to where Kate, for a moment by herself, was making a half-hearted attempt to tidy the table.

'Lovely evening, Kate,' he said. 'Funny, isn't it, how we all work together every day, and yet find so much to talk about when we meet like this?' He waved a hand round the room.

He topped up Kate's glass and then his own. 'Bella's turn to drive,' he explained. He gave her a long look from his dark brown intelligent eyes. 'The bombing and Jonathan's injury must have been hell for you, Kate. Would you believe we feel quite guilty for being away at the time? It's ridiculous, isn't it, this guilt thing that most of us have for something we can't help?'

'That's why Rory suggested the help-yourself evenings for anyone to come to, however remotely they were connected with the bombing. A lot of people have said exactly what you have about feeling guilty. That's why we're going to discuss a permanent arrangement at the monthly staff meeting—try to cover a wider field of trauma. I doubt that we will ever have anything so dramatic to cope with, but people are suffering from varying degrees of loss and guilt all the time.'

'I think it's a brilliant idea. More talk, less tranquillisers; a bit of extra effort once a week might save time and distress in the end. Great bloke, Rory—pity he's only passing through, as it were. But no chance of a high-flyer like him settling down as a humble GP. We're going to miss him when he goes, Kate, aren't we?'

It was a statement, not a question. Kate felt the hairs stand up on the back of her neck. Mike knows, she realised; he knows or has guessed about Rory and me. She met Mike's eyes and saw that they were full of compassion.

They were joined by Dr North senior. 'We'll be off now, Kate; I'm sorry to drag Jonathan away at what probably seems an early hour to you youngsters, but I'm a frail, decrepit invalid, and looking forward to my bed.'

'Get away with you, Matt,' said Mike. 'An old

workhorse like you.' He gave the older man an affectionate punch on the shoulder. 'But you're right about
bed; I've a busy day tomorrow.'

He went away to collect Bella, and Kate told
Jonathan that his father wanted to go home. Somehow
she got through the chore of seeing everyone off and
helping her mother to bed by means of blocking out
the fact that Mike knew about her and Rory.

She persuaded Dora, who looked very tired, to let
her tidy away and do the washing up, suggesting that
Jonathan might well return to say goodnight. 'And he
would much rather find me on my own,' she offered as
an excuse, which Dora readily understood.

On her own at last, carrying dirty dishes through to
the kitchen, Kate went over and over that moment
with Mike. It was astonishing. Without actually saying
so, Mike had made it plain that he knew more than a
little, carefully linking their conversation about guilt,
the meetings and Rory together.

She finished clearing up and went to bed. A sudden
thought made her sit up with a jerk. Was it possible
that Rory had said or indicated something about his
feelings to Mike? No, of course not. He wouldn't
dream of doing such a thing even though he and Mike
had quickly established a rapport. To start with, she
and Rory had only just revealed their feelings to each
other, and it was unthinkable that he would discuss her
with someone else.

The night had grown humid and uncomfortable.
Kate tossed and turned, tormented by her mixed-up
thoughts and suspicions. She fell at last into an uneasy
sleep, to dream of Rory, Jonathan and Mike. They
were all stripped to the waist, with their trousers rolled
up and their torsos gleaming with sweat in the light of
red flames. They seemed to be digging, though it wasn't
clear that they were wielding spades. The picture
dissolved, and against a background of orange light

they swayed and pawed at each other like old-time wrestlers.

The dream-cum-nightmare stopped suddenly as she woke to find the light from a full harvest moon shining through the curtains. She sighed, trying to remember her dream, but it had sunk without trace.

She sat up, punched her pillows venomously, turned on her side and fell fast asleep till morning.

She had only been in the centre a few minutes the following morning, when Rory phoned on the internal line.

'I have to go up to town for a few days,' he said. 'Jonathan knows about it. We have sorted out cover while I'm away.' His voice dropped an octave. 'My dear, I wanted to talk to you about this, but haven't had an opportunity. Can you meet me for lunch, say at the Castle Arms?'

His voice made Kate's pulses race. She dithered. 'I don't know; perhaps. What about Jonathan?'

'What about Jonathan? I'm only suggesting lunch, all open and above board, two colleagues meeting, not an orgy.'

There was a suggestion of laughter in his voice, but Kate had the impression that he was deadly serious.

'Right, I'll see you at about one o'clock.' She remembered Jonathan saying something about the flesh-pots of Harley Street. Was this where Rory was heading?

She put her personal problems aside to concentrate on professional matters. There was a whole pile of forms already on her desk, mostly blood tests requested by the doctors on duty yesterday, referring to patients booked in this morning. She would be lucky to get through them all without interruption. Most mornings one or the other of the doctors on duty wanted her to do a test of some sort in a hurry.

True to form, the phone rang before she'd even called in the first patient. It was Rachel.

'Kate.' She sounded urgent. 'Did you know that Miss West—Dora—was booked in to see me this morning?'

'Dora? No, of course I didn't. She usually sees Dr North senior, most of the older patients do. Since he's been ill they've either see Jonathan or Rory.'

'Well, apparently she wanted to see me in particular. I understand Rory persuaded her to make an appointment. She's got a mild vaginal discharge and a touch of pruritus vulva, which explains why I am the flavour of the month, being the only woman medic in the practice. She's run down, very thirsty, tired and putting out large quantities of urine. She said that she would have asked your advice, but didn't want to worry you. As you can see, she's exhibiting all the signs of diabetus mellitus. Will you do the usual blood and urine tests, please, as soon as possible? I've sent her back to the waiting-room, and warned her that she will be seeing you. Apparently she didn't realise that you would have to know. She wanted to save you the worry of everything.'

Kate was shocked and disgusted with herself for not having noticed Dora's problem. She felt dreadfully guilty. Even after her mother had suggested a week or so ago that Dora was off colour, she'd not done anything about it. Well, she had asked Dora when she got home how she felt, but had accepted her answer of 'having a touch of the summer flu' as the problem. Yet Rory, on one of his visits to Bathurst, must have guessed at her not being well and persuaded her to see Rachel.

How could you be so bloody selfish? she asked herself. She sat down at her desk and, uncharacteristically, burst into tears.

She didn't even hear the tap at the door, but was suddenly aware of Rory being in the room. He put a hand on her shoulder and squeezed it gently. 'Kate, tell me what's wrong,' he said.

She raised her head and looked up at him through bleary, tear-stained eyes, neither knowing, nor caring, that she looked a fright. 'I'm so damned selfish,' she said in a wobbly voice. 'Poor Dora, she's ill, has been for weeks and I haven't even noticed it.'

'You've had a lot on your mind: your mother, Thomas, the bombing, and of course Jonathan, and you've kept this place ticking over. Give yourself a break, my dear, stop martyring yourself. You're only human.' His mouth quirked in a gentle smile, and his eyes were full of tenderness and understanding.

'But you could see that Dora wasn't well; why couldn't I?'

'Partly because of all the things that I have mentioned, partly because you see her daily and are less likely to notice gradual changes. But most of all, I suspect, because Dora didn't want you to know that she wasn't feeling well. She loves you, Kate, and wanted to spare you any more worry.'

He moved behind her and started to massage her neck and shoulders. 'My dearest girl, you're all knotted up,' he breathed softly. 'Relax now, don't resist. Five minutes will make all the difference.'

Kate gave in and let him gently pummel her rigid muscles. She began to feel less tense. 'What did you come in for?' she asked.

'Just to see you,' was his astonishing reply. 'I couldn't wait till lunchtime. Jonathan's gone off on early rounds.'

She had to ask. 'What am I to do about Jonathan? I hate deceiving him.' She thought of another reason to be cautious. 'And you and I, we hardly know each other, and yet we're behaving as if. . .'

'As if?'

'You seem so sure about——'

'Loving you, Kate?'

She nodded. He bent and kissed her bowed head. 'But I am, my love. I'm thirty-eight, and I know that this is the real thing. You need time to think about it, not just because of Jonathan, although he is, of course, your chief reason for caution, but for many other reasons. I can be patient when I have to. I can wait; in fact I'd rather. Don't feel pressurised, Kate. It's the last thing I want you to be. When you reach a decision about us, I hope that it will be firm, unequivocal, without guilty overtones. Take your time, love, I can wait,' he repeated.

'I do love you,' she whispered. 'It's just that everything seems so complicated. Jonathan needs me, and he. . .Well, you of all people.'

Rory looked grim. 'I know, he hates me. An irrational emotion that has bugged him for years. For his sake, love, we must bide our time. We must both be patient. You do realise,' he said, 'that he is not a well man, don't you?'

'But he's getting better, every day.'

'Yes, at present, but he's an unstable personality— you must have seen that? Quite apart from his unexplained period of unconsciousness after his injury, there have been other signs.'

The telephone rang. It was an outside call. 'Kate, has Dora seen you yet?' asked Mrs Christy. 'I only realised this morning that she was going to the surgery to see Rachel.'

Kate pulled herself together. This was her work; nothing would stop her from doing her duty. 'I'm just going to see Dora now,' she told her mother. 'Rachel wants me to do some tests.'

'Has she got diabetes, Kate?'

'I don't know for sure, not until the results of the tests are known.'

Her mother sounded exasperated. 'Afraid to commit

yourself, Kate? It wouldn't have happened in the old days; your father would have known if it was diabetes or something else.'

'Well, to start with, I'm not a doctor, and anyway, we're not allowed to guess these days,' said Kate firmly. 'I'll let you know as soon as we have any news. Goodbye.' She slapped the receiver down and looked at Rory. 'What have I done?' she whispered.

'Told the plain, unvarnished truth,' he replied. 'You can't go on protecting everyone all the time, my darling.'

Her heart bounded with pleasure at his endearment, but it didn't stop her feeling guilty about being sharp with her mother, or her neglect of Dora.

'I must get on,' she said. 'I've a load of bloods and other things to do.'

'You'd better go and wash your face before you start seeing patients.' Rory pulled her to her feet and led her towards the clinic-room. He pushed her gently through the door. 'Go on, make yourself presentable; I'll see you at lunchtime.'

It wasn't as harrowing as she had expected, dealing with Dora. In fact, it was Dora who was full of remorse for not having asked Kate's advice earlier.

'I feel so guilty,' she said, 'thinking it was a kindness not to worry you, and now look what's happened!' She waved her hand round the clinic-room, indicating all the various bits of machinery and instruments, bottles and syringes, as if these inanimate objects were responsible for her problems. 'I'm so sorry, Kate, to have kept you in the dark, but I did it for the best.' She looked sad and crestfallen.

'But you would have had to have these same tests whenever you had decided to confide in someone, Dora, whether it was now or weeks ago. The doctors have yet to diagnose what's wrong with you, and they

can only do that after the results of certain tests on
your blood are known.'

'And you're not cross because I didn't tell you
sooner?'

'Not a bit cross. I just wish that I'd noticed earlier
what was happening and done something about it.'

Dora hooted with laughter, and Kate was cheered
by her instant reaction. 'What, you with all the dependants hanging on to your coat-tails? Don't be daft; how
could you be expected to see me getting a bit worse for
wear? What I'm concerned about is how soon I'm
going to get treated for whatever's wrong with me, and
get back to doing a proper day's work. Now, can you
tell me that?'

'No, I can't, but I don't think that you'll be out of
action too long. Basically you're very fit; that's going
to be a help. But you must be prepared to go into
hospital for a day or two. If you have diabetes, you will
need to be stabilised on a diet and or medication.'

'Tablets, you mean—I'm not going to be needing
injections and things, am I?' For the first time Dora
sounded nervous.

Kate answered truthfully, 'I don't know, Dora. It's
not even certain, although it seems probable, that you
have diabetes. If you have, it might be controlled just
through diet, or you might need medication in other
forms to help you with your sugar balance.'

She was preparing to take a blood sample and
fastening the tourniquet cuff round Dora's upper arm.

'I'm just going to take some blood from here.' She
indicated the blood-vessel inside the elbow. 'And to do
this I need to put pressure here.' She tightened the cuff
round the upper arm. She made it a routine to explain
exactly what she was going to do to all patients. 'Now,
clench your fist, please, Dora. That's fine.' Kate
inserted the needle easily into the distended blood-
vessel and drew up a sufficient amount of blood for the

various tests that she had to make. 'Right, unclench now.' She released the cuff and put a piece of cotton wool over the small puncture left in the skin. 'Keep your elbow bent and that in position for a minute or so,' she instructed.

Dora did as she was told. 'Your dad would have been proud of you, Kate,' she said a bit later. 'Why didn't you go in for medicine instead of nursing?' she asked. 'I've always wondered.

'Because I wanted to be a nurse, not a doctor,' replied Kate. 'It's just as important as medicine, you know. Only different.'

'Yes,' said Dora, 'I suppose it is.' She sounded a bit doubtful, but Kate couldn't think of any further arguments in favour of nursing at the moment and she had a room full of patients waiting to be seen.

She gave Dora a specimen-pot as she was leaving. 'It's to pass urine into,' she explained. 'First thing in the morning if you can. I'll bring it into the surgery tomorrow for testing.'

'I did that for Dr Lyons,' she said, sounding quite indignant. 'Passed water, she tested it.'

'Yes,' said Kate patiently. 'But I want you to do an early-morning specimen, that's the most accurate. Please Dora, it's the usual procedure.'

'Oh, all right, anything to please you,' returned Dora with a grin. 'You know, things were much simpler in your father's day. He would probably have known what was wrong with me without all this bother.'

'Perhaps,' said Kate, smiling. 'But he would still have done these tests. They've been around for a long time.'

The phone rang as the next patient was coming into the clinic-room. It was Rory.

'I'm so sorry, Kate,' he said. 'I have to cancel our luncheon date. I'm going up to town as soon as I've finished my rounds. Jonathan knows about it.'

He put the phone down, leaving her no time to question him. Had anything at this end happened to make him change his mind, she wondered, or had he had a sudden emergency call from his consulting rooms in Harley Street?

A few minutes later, Jonathan phoned. 'Let's go out for lunch,' he suggested jubilantly. 'I've got something special to say to you.'

'Really?' Kate said, drawing a deep breath and wondering if he knew that Rory had been going to take her to lunch. He sounded very elated and self-assured. Could this have anything to do with Rory going away? 'All right, where shall we go?'

Usually, he was hesitant about making any decision, even something as trivial as where to eat. On this occasion he said at once, 'The Kettle of Fish.'

'OK, about one o'clock.'

'Great,' said Jonathan. 'See you then, darling.'

Kate put down the phone, and sat for a few minutes staring at it and puzzling over Jonathan's ebullience. It was a long time since he had been so decisive and sure of himself. If he was regaining some of his former confidence it would make her task easier when the time came to speak of her feelings for Rory.

The Kettle of Fish was a pretty thatched pub about a mile out of town on the edge of the river. Because of its chocolate-box prettiness it attracted a large passing trade from tourists. But it also had a regular clientele of executive types drawn from the nearby exclusive estate, and the wealthier local farmers. Many of these were patients as well as friends.

Kate was surprised that Jonathan had chosen this particular pub for their meeting, and relieved, too. The last thing she wanted after her distressing morning was a confrontation with Jonathan. Well, she consoled herself, that wasn't likely to happen; this place was much too public.

Perhaps that augured well for their get-together. Maybe Jonathan wanted a less intimate meal. He had seemed relaxed and happy last night at the supper party, and his mood when he phoned had been remarkably cheerful. Perhaps this was what he wanted to celebrate—perhaps he was aware of the change in himself, and wanted to share it with her.

It was a wonderful, comforting thought, if only he could hang on to this more stable frame of mind. So often over the last year or so his moods had changed like lightning. He had been totally unpredictable. She prayed that today he would be as happy when they met as when he had phoned.

He was. He was waiting for her in the car park and came forward to greet her with open arms, taking both her hands in his, and bending to give her a loving kiss on her cheek.

He looked marvellous, Kate thought. Last night she had been struck by his improved appearance and his less guarded manner, but today there was an added quality, an aura of well-being that was quite new to him. His hair looked healthy and glossy and the small beard which he was growing to replace the one shaved off when he was injured seemed suddenly to have become an elegant, fine-looking 'imperial'. His eyes, too, were remarkably clear and bright. But above all it was his confident manner that was most impressive.

For the first time in a long while he emanated a quiet and charming confidence. Kate was enchanted. She hadn't seen him like this for years. Confidence, in fact, seemed the key to the change in him.

He steered her into the restaurant end of the pub. 'Window table,' he said, guiding her to it while nodding to or having a word with friends at other tables.

Well, she thought, whatever news he has to impart

he certainly doesn't mean to keep secret. The table he had chosen was the most prominent in the room.

As they reached it, Lawrence Rider, the owner and manager of the pub, materialised in time to pull out a chair for Kate. She thanked him with a smile, and took her place opposite Jonathan, almost a stranger, the other side of the table.

'Ready?' Lawrence asked Jonathan.

'Ready. Bring on the champers, Lawrence.'

'Champagne?' queried Kate. 'At lunchtime? Jonathan, I have to drive back and work this afternoon.'

'Darling, if necessary I'll arrange to have your car driven back to the centre and we can take a taxi. And, since you must work, you can soak up a great wine with great food. This is a celebration.'

'My goodness, it must be special, the occasion.'

'Oh, it is, Kate, and I hope that you are going to make it doubly special. A double reason for celebrating.'

Lawrence returned with the champagne resplendent in a silver ice-bucket. He removed the cork with the subdued pop only produced by a good vintage and proceeded, at a nod from Jonathan, to pour the wine before going discreetly away.

'Will you join me in a toast, Kate?' Jonathan lifted his glass towards her. She raised hers.

'It might help,' she said, with a little smile, eager to join him in his obvious delight in the moment, 'if you tell me what we are toasting.'

He laughed. A lovely natural laugh, full of innocent pleasure. She hadn't heard him laugh this way for a long, long time. Her smile broadened. 'Well?'

'Will you please drink to the new head of practice, Kate?' He clinked his glass against her glass, and leaned across the table so that his face was close to hers. 'I'm going to be your boss, my darling, in the very near future. Now, isn't that something to celebrate?'

Kate sat still as a statue, her glass resting against his, her eyes meeting his across the few inches of space that was between them. For one tiny moment she thought, hoped, that she might have misheard him, but she knew instinctively that that was wishful thinking. 'Head of practice!' she exclaimed through stiff lips. 'Head of practice?' she repeated.

Jonathan grinned widely. 'That's what I said, my darling—head—of—practice,' he repeated, mouthing each word slowly and emphatically, as if she were deaf. He was delighted with her obvious amazement. 'Isn't it wonderful? Come on, darling, drink up, congratulate me. Be pleased for me.' For a moment he looked a little anxious. 'You are pleased for me, Kate, aren't you, that I should take over from Dad?'

Somehow she made herself smile and then take a sip of the wine. 'Of course I am, Jonathan, absolutely delighted; congratulations.' It sounded weak and very low key, certainly not matching his state of euphoria. To ginger it up, she added, 'A thousand congratulations, dear Jonathan. I'm so happy for you.'

He seemed satisfied with this and leaned back in his chair, beaming at her across the table. 'I've ordered the meal,' he said, revelling in his new-found confidence. 'All the things that I know you like.'

Kate just nodded, unable to make any further noises of approbation.

'So your father has plans to retire?' she said after a while, groping for information.

'Of course; I wouldn't be taking over otherwise, darling, would I?'

'No, of course not. It's just that he's not given any indication that he means to do so. Only last night he was talking about returning to part-time work soon. When did he make this decision to retire?'

'Funnily enough, it was on the way back from your house last night.'

'But something as important as this needs a lot of discussion; you haven't had time to talk about it properly, surely? You were doing rounds until a short while ago.'

For the first time Jonathan looked a little less than certain of himself. 'But we did talk; I've just come from home. And this afternoon I'll finish my rounds while Rachel covers my clinic.'

'But she's got an afternoon off; she needs it, Jonathan, she worked so hard——'

'When I was living it up, unconscious on a hospital bed?' He sounded very sarcastic.

Kate was determined that he shouldn't lose his present confidence. 'Oh, darling, I am sorry, how stupid of me. Of course it won't hurt her to work an hour or two extra, especially in such a good cause.' She smiled at him, a gentle, loving smile that completely reassured him.

He leaned forward. 'And you can make it a perfect occasion,' he said quietly. 'Remember I said that there would be a second reason to celebrate?'

Kate nodded.

'Well,' he went on, 'what better timing could we have to announce our forthcoming engagement than now? Kate, you will marry me, won't you?'

She felt as if she had been hit by a sledge-hammer. She found it hard to hear and then appreciate what he was saying. He took hold of her hand.

'Kate,' he said. 'I should have asked you ages ago, but didn't have the courage. Will you marry me?'

Words came at last. 'No,' she said. 'No. How dare you ask me now in front of a roomful of people? No, I won't marry you.' It was her turn to lean across the table. 'Get me out of here,' she gritted. 'Now, at once.'

In shocked silence, Jonathan guided her from the

room, a hand beneath her elbow, murmuring professional excuses to their host.

In the car park, aware of the interested gaze of many of the customers, she reached up and kissed him. 'This is just for show,' she told him coldly, through clenched teeth. 'It means nothing.'

She got into her car and drove away. In her mirror she could see him looking lost, alone, and somehow pathetic. . .

CHAPTER NINE

KATE drove with extra care back to the centre. She knew that her tumultuous thoughts and ferocious temper were a hazard to driving and she must contain herself. Anger, after alcohol, was one of the main causes of accidents.

The weather conditions didn't help. There had been a light shower while she and Jonathan were in the restaurant, producing greasy patches on the previously dry-as-dust surface. Handfuls of brilliantly coloured autumn leaves adhered to the road, looking beautiful, but dangerous. The wind blew in great gusts, tossing the branches of trees, tearing off leaves, scattering wet straw-dust from the harvested fields. Yet in spite of the rain and wind it remained humid and uncomfortably warm for early October.

In fact, the weather seemed to mirror her situation: euphoric, almost tropically perfect one moment, unutterably depressing and grey with drizzle the next. Never serene and comfortable.

What, she asked herself, as she safely drew into the health centre's forecourt, was she to do about Jonathan? She was already regretting her hurried departure from the restaurant, for many reasons, some quite selfish, others out of concern for him. She had no wish to make him look foolish in front of friends or acquaintances. With luck, they might put her precipitate departure down to a professional call.

If only Rory were here to talk to, she might make some sense out of the situation. As it was, she not only didn't have his support, but didn't even know if he had left in a hurry because of the situation. Not, she reminded herself, that he would run away from a problem. He would meet it head on, with courage, calm and logic. That was some sort of comfort.

She whisked through the waiting-room, just filling up with afternoon patients, throwing out greetings as she went. No one, she determined, was going to know from her attitude that she was in the grip of a crisis of despair.

The phone was ringing in her office as she opened the door. It was Rory. Her spirits soared at the sound of his voice, deep and tender. 'Dear Kate,' he said softly. 'You must be wondering why I left in such a hurry this morning.'

'Yes, though I presumed that you had an emergency at the London end.'

'At both ends, my dear—Midchester and London.'

'Jonathan?'

'How did you know?'

'I've just come back from seeing him. Rory, do you know if it's true that your uncle is retiring and handing over to Jonathan?'

'I'm not sure. Uncle Matt rang me just after I'd asked you to meet me for lunch this morning. He was somewhat distressed. I went home to see him as soon as I could. You had patients with you, so I didn't disturb you; I thought that I'd be back to explain later.'

'What happened, for heaven's sake?'

'I'm still not sure. Uncle Matt, for once, and quite out of character, seemed muddled. He asked me to make myself scarce for a few days while he sorted out matters between him and Jonathan. It seemed sensible; I'd finished surgery, Mike agreed to do my visits—it was really no problem to leave at once. But what he wanted to say to Jonathan, I don't know. I can't think, though, that he would contemplate handing over to him. He knows that it would be a disaster. I doubt that Mike would stand for it anyway.'

Some perverse stirrings of loyalty made Kate say sharply, 'Perhaps what Jonathan needs is to be trusted by his father. It was always understood that he would inherit the role of head of practice one day. I'm sure that Mike Dolland knew that when he came to work here.'

Rory was silent for a few moments. Then he said quietly, 'You may be right, Kate. Perhaps my cousin needs to know that he is appreciated in the right quarters. Maybe it would be the making of him.'

Kate was already questioning her spontaneous defence of Jonathan. He wasn't ready for leadership, and, in her heart of hearts, she knew that he never would be. Even the display at the Kettle of Fish, when he had seemed so normal, was not a true picture. It was like looking in a trick mirror—sometimes the image looked like an accurate reflection, sometimes it looked distorted, and a move of a few inches could cause a change in perspective. That, if one was honest, summed up Jonathan North.

'Rory, I——'

He interrupted, perhaps anticipating her retraction. 'No, Kate, you're right. Jonathan must be given a chance to respond to the challenge, if that's what Uncle Matt has in mind. Give him all the support that you can. He'll need you, my dear.'

'But you——'

'Yes, I need you too, Kate, but, without sounding conceited, may I suggest that his need is greater than mine?'

She was horrified. What was he saying—that he was willing to sever their just budding relationship to accommodate Jonathan? Was he asking her to enter into an arrangement with his cousin for some noble family reasons? Perhaps he was using her to assuage his guilt of years before, when he had walked out on his uncle. Provoked he might have been, but he had departed and left his Uncle Matt devastated by his departure.

It seemed, when one came down to it, that his love for her, on which she would have banked her life only hours before, was in fact dispensable. Blood, it seemed, was indeed thicker than water. He was willing to trade their mutual affection for the well-being of his uncle and the possible rehabilitation of his cousin.

Kate felt sick with fury. The man whom she had been prepared to depend upon was no more reliable than Jonathan, it seemed. And, she thought, emotion blinding her to all else, with less excuse. He had all his faculties and abilities going full tilt, whereas Jonathan, poor darling, was hampered, by nature or by some impairment of intellect, from fulfilling himself. At least he genuinely loved her, wanted to marry her. Success in his profession went hand in hand with his desire for her companionship.

In a resigned fashion, she realised that Jonathan had been right all along. Rory's arrival had caused havoc with everything. Jonathan had been right to be worried that his charismatic cousin would steal everything from him. Dr North senior's affection, the practice, and her affection too—well, nearly, but she wasn't going to let that happen. She was full of remorse.

Mustering all her moral courage, she said in a cool voice, 'Yes, I think you must be right, Rory. He hasn't really been given a chance to prove himself. You've always been there, the perfect example of a perfect doctor, and his father has always had the love as well as the respect of his patients. While Jonathan——' she swallowed a lump of misery in her throat '—poor Jonathan has had to battle to be just an average doctor, and against the tide of his mother's smothering. You're absolutely right; he needs me if only because I want to make up to him for what he's missed.'

She heard Rory breathe in sharply, but before he

could speak again she added, 'Thank you very much for making things clear, Rory; I'll say goodbye now. Patients waiting.' Gently she put down the receiver. 'Well,' she said, looking round her office with unseeing eyes, 'that's that.'

As if in a dream she went through to the clinic-room and consulted the list of patients booked to see her that afternoon.

There were several injections to do. Iron for Miss Connell, who had an aversion to the district nurses and insisted on coming to the surgery. Maintenance sub-cutaneous injections for the twin brothers Kevin and Tony Foster still suffering from a hay-fever-like con-dition, prolonged because of the long, hot summer. Throat swabs from the Black family, in an attempt to isolate a bug which was giving them all sore throats as yet unresponsive to various remedies. Two leg ulcers to be checked and re-dressed, and stitches to be removed from a foot wound.

Like an automaton, but keeping up a flow of incon-sequential conversation, Kate worked her way through the list. Miss Connell, iron deficiency, a 5M1.I.M.I. of Jectofer, to be given carefully, making sure that the needle was clear and surrounding tissue not discoloured.

Then the Blacks, five of them. They all submitted quietly enough to the gentle touch with the long-stemmed swabs, all, that was except Mr Black, who gagged and coughed even before Kate had touched his throat. The Black children thought this was a great joke, and fell about laughing. Kate suggested that Mrs Black took them through to the waiting-room while she dealt with their father on his own.

Mr Black was grateful. 'I've always had a ticklish sort of throat, Sister,' he explained. 'And of course it seemed worse in front of the kids. I think I'll be all right now.'

Kate was successful after the second try, to his great relief. 'Will you ask the Foster boys to come in, please?' she asked as he was leaving.

The Foster twins bounced in just as she was completing the labels on the throat-swab tubes. They came regularly every few weeks for their maintenance shots of Spectralgen Tree, an allergen prepared from three tree pollens. Because of their regular visits over a long period, they felt quite at home in the clinic-room. At thirteen years old they were boisterous and inclined to be cheeky, but not rude.

Usually Kate was pleased to see them, for they brought a breath of normality into the health centre, but today she felt that she could do without their continuous commentary.

Her irritation was obvious and Kevin, the eldest by a few minutes, nudged Tony, and said with heavy significance, 'Somebody's in a bad mood, then, aren't they?'

Tony, the more sensitive of the two, looked uncomfortable. 'Shut up, Kev,' he said. 'Sister's entitled to be a bit off if she wants to be.'

Their comments rattled Kate. Entitled she might be, but not when on duty. Her time and temperament belonged then to the patients. No way was she going to break the habit of her professional life and let personal matters intrude.

'Do you mind?' she said in a jokey fashion. 'I'm just concentrating.'

'Oh, is that what it is, Sister? Excuse me for making a mistake.' Kev grinned cheerfully, prepared to accept her word for it, though Kate wasn't sure he quite believed her.

Hot on the twins' heels came the two leg ulcers, one after another. One was healing nicely and Kate renewed the dressing, this time to be left on for a longer period. 'I don't expect to see you back for a week, Mr Scott,' she told the old gentleman, who looked at her with vacant, rheumy eyes.

'Eh?' he said.

'Is your wife with you?' Kate asked gently. He nodded. 'I'll have a word with her,' she said, steering him back to the waiting-room. She explained to Mrs Scott about there being no need for her husband to come for at least a week.

'There, Reg, that's good news, isn't it? Now you just sit there and I'll make an appointment for next week, then we'll go and pick up a nice bit of fish for our tea.' She smiled at Kate. 'He likes a nice bit of fish,' she said.

Kate took a few deep breaths when she returned to the clinic-room. Why are some people so nice? she asked herself. They've got so little to look forward to, and yet. . . Her thoughts trailed away and she reminded herself that she'd better get on with her work.

The second ulcer was not healing at all well. Mike Dolland had scrawled a note for Kate.

Will you try the new dressing pack left by the rep from Abbots? Might help—if that doesn't work, looks like surgery.

Kate explained to Mrs Craine that she was going to try a new dressing. 'Oh, well, anything you say, Sister; I'm not fussy. I just want to get the wretched thing cleared up.' She looked anxious for a moment. 'It will clear up, Sister, won't it—in time, I mean?'

'Well, the new dressing has properties in it that we haven't tried before. Dr Dolland wants us to give it a go. If it doesn't work, he might suggest that you see a surgeon with a view to having a skin graft over the ulcerated area.'

'An operation, you mean, Sister?' Mrs Craine sounded horrified. 'I've never been in hospital. It seems silly, just for this.' She pointed at the ulcer.

'Well, let's hope that it won't be necessary. This new dressing may do the trick.'

There was a short gap between Mrs Craine's departing and Lewis Cartwright's arriving to have the stitches removed from his foot wound. He was cheerful and optimistic about being back on his feet in time for a skating competition.

Kate, having removed the stitches from a long gash in the sole of his foot, was able to confirm that, given a week or two, his foot would be as good as new.

Lewis looked a bit shy. 'Will you take these, Sister?' he asked, thrusting two pieces of card into her hand. 'They're tickets for the final of "Skating South", which I'm entered for in November. If I win I go through to the nationals in December.'

'I'd love to come,' said Kate, pocketing the tickets, touched by his enthusiasm.

'Bring your boyfriend,' said Lewis, as he hopped out of the room.

Mechanically, Kate began to tidy up the room after Lewis, who was her last patient, had gone. She put instruments in to the steriliser, tidied away dressing packs, made sure that all dirty syringes were made unusable and needles fed into the 'sharps' container.

She was wiping down surfaces with cleaning spirit when there was a knock at the door.

'Come in,' she called, thinking that it was probably Potty wanting to check off her list for tomorrow. 'Won't be a minute,' she said, and crouched down to swab over a glass shelf on the dressings trolley.

Rory said, speaking from where he was standing just inside the door, 'My dear girl, I'm so glad that you're finished for the day; may we now finish our conversation?'

Kate straightened up slowly and stared at him. She

felt her cheeks go hot. 'What are you doing here? You're in London,' she said in a stony voice.

'An hour and a half away,' he replied. 'As for what I'm doing. . .' he shrugged '. . .trying to mend broken fences.'

'I shouldn't bother.' Somehow, Kate thought, I must hang on to my pride. I must not cave in at the first suggestion. . . Of what? she asked herself. What is Rory suggesting by being here? He says 'mending fences', but what does he mean by that? 'I don't know what you mean,' she said, with difficulty, getting the words out from a throat that ached with unshed tears.

'I mean, dear girl, that I don't want any misunderstandings between you and me.'

Kate looked at him leaning against the wall beside the door. He was wearing a dark charcoal-grey suit, white silk shirt and a discreet Paisley-patterned silk tie. Consultant's uniform. His bronze-blond hair, peppered with grey above his ears, had been cut since she'd commented on the need for a trim weeks before. It seemed incredible that he should have bothered to make the trip back from town, not long after arriving there, and just to see her. Could it be true?

Her heart thudded painfully. She forced herself to look away from him. She picked up an odd swab and scrap of paper that had missed the bin.

'I don't think that there has been any misunderstanding,' she said icily. 'You made everything crystal-clear when you phoned earlier.'

'No, you cut me off, remember?'

'After what you said, you implied. . . What do you think I am, a pawn in the North family's game? How generous of you to hand me over to your more needy cousin. Well, you don't have to persuade me to marry Jonathan; it was always on the cards that I should do so, but you almost mucked it up for both of us. Only understand this—I've made my decision, and it has nothing to do with your persuasive tongue.'

Her own tongue seemed to have run away with the words, which just spilled out. She knew that she shouldn't be saying so much, but she just couldn't stop. Rory's presence triggered off all the pent-up emotions of the day. She slumped down on a chair, feeling as limp as a rag-doll, and buried her face in her hands. She couldn't even cry.

Rory crossed the room in a few easy strides, and stood in front of her. Very softly he said, 'Kate, I don't know how you interpreted what I said earlier, or what you thought I meant, but it was certainly not a suggestion that you should marry Jonathan. Give him your time and friendship, yes, let him down gently, perhaps even delay making any overt changes in your relationship, but not marriage, Kate, not marriage.'

Dry-eyed, she looked up at him and said tonelessly, 'I don't know what to make of you, Rory. How can you say that you love me and yet not mind my being close to Jonathan?'

'I didn't say that I didn't mind.'

'Well, as good as.'

'No, my dear, in fact I mind very much. But I'm concerned for Jonathan and for my uncle and at the present time you are the sheet-anchor for both of them.'

'It's you your uncle depends upon, not me.' She was beyond surprise, infinitely weary. She wished the conversation would end and Rory would go away.

'But he believes, at this moment in time anyway, that you're the key to Jonathan's well-being. He said as much, and he wants to protect his only son. I think that's why he sent me away, just to give Jonathan enough time to act positively. The old boy's very perceptive. I think he guessed about us and——'

There was a knock at the door, and before Kate

could answer Jonathan walked into the room. He
hesitated just inside the door when he saw Rory. 'What
the hell are you doing here?' he asked abruptly. 'I
thought you were in Harley Street.'

For once, Rory seemed a little uncomfortable but
quickly regained his equilibrium and replied easily,
'Came back to fetch something as I left in rather a
hurry. Thought I'd look in on Kate and fill her in on
some patients I want to see when I get back at the end
of the week.'

'Will you be back at the end of the week? I thought
you were returning to town for good.'

'Oh, no, I'll be staying in town for three days each
week, but I'll stay around to give a hand as needed
until Uncle's back in harness.'

'Then you'll have to stay around for a long time,
dear cousin—Dad's not coming back to work. At least,
only occasionally to do a locum.' He thrust his face
forward, almost into Rory's. His eyes glittered. 'It'll be
up to head of practice who comes and goes to help
out,' he said in a voice heavy with sarcasm. 'And that
means me, and I can tell you right now that your
services will not be required.'

The two men stood there belligerently facing each
other. This must be a bad dream, thought Kate,
looking at their angry faces. Even Rory seemed to have
lost his usual calm and was looking at Jonathan with a
mixture of intense dislike and despair. Two sides of his
persona battling. Which would win, Kate wondered in
a detached way, Rory the man or Rory the physician?

There was a knock at the door, which was opened
before Kate could answer. It was Mike.

'Oh, hello,' he said amiably, seeing only the three of
them, and not immediately picking up any bad vibes.
He looked at Rory. 'Thought you were up in town at
your rooms?' he remarked, sounding slightly surprised.

'Forgot something, had to come back,' replied Rory briskly.

His briskness warned Mike that something was wrong. 'Look,' he said looking uncomfortable, 'would it be better if——'

'Yes,' cut in Rory, continuing to sound abrupt. He added a little less tersely, 'Family matter; I'm sure you understand.'

Mike looked uncertainly from one to the other. A shaft of stormy sunshine cut through one of the windows, bathing the three men in its orange glow. Kate felt as if she was watching an old movie that she'd seen before, and it was that hazy memory, full of foreboding, that made her speak at last.

In a very cold voice that made them all turn and look at her, she said, 'No, it's not just a family matter, it's a practice matter too. We should all talk this over.'

Both Rory and Jonathan looked astonished and outraged. For a moment, Kate glimpsed a family likeness as they momentarily became allies in defence of their family name. They began to protest simultaneously, but Kate was firm. She was wholly on the side of the practice, if necessary against both of them, and she would even take up arms against old Dr North if the situation called for it.

Mike still seemed to be out of his depth, looking from one to the other of them and then back to Kate, clearly embarrassed. 'Look, Kate,' he muttered. 'Don't worry about me—we can talk things over later.'

'You're a partner, for God's sake, Mike. Don't you want to protect your interests and the interest of the practice?'

'Of course, but I don't see——'

'Well, stick around and you will,' she interrupted savagely. 'Don't walk away and leave these two to use a personal, long-standing feud to smash up everything that their family has built up over several generations.'

She was amazed at her own temerity. But some inner strength and an odd feeling of relief that she was at last able to do something constructive, rather than be blown along haphazardly like the autumn leaves, gave her courage.

Mike visibly pulled himself together and turned to face Rory and Jonathan. 'If what Kate says is true, and of course I believe her, then I deserve to know more of what's going on. But I can't stop now, and neither can you, Jonathan—we've both got evening surgery.'

Jonathan was looking deflated, quite unlike the confident man who had taken Kate out to lunch and boasted of the position that was soon to be his. Head hung down, he growled into his beard, 'Rachel—Rachel's covering for me.'

'No, she ain't, mate,' said Mike trying to instil some humour into the situation. 'She's gone home. Thought she was here just to cover your afternoon clinic. You're stuck with a surgery, old son, however much you resent it.'

For once Mike sounded a bit fed up, and Kate realised that he too had covered a lot for Jonathan since the bombing. In fact he'd done more than his fair share, probably trying to kill his guilt feelings for being absent when Midchester's greatest emergency hit town. And Jonathan had been only too willing to take advantage of the situation.

Rory spoke for the first time since Kate's outburst. He stretched out and put a hand on her shoulder. 'Thanks, Kate,' he said in a low but clear voice. 'Jonathan and I owe you a great deal. Things were getting out of hand. Thanks for putting the brakes on.'

Kate simply nodded; for the life of her she couldn't think of anything more to say or do. But after a moment she did find some silly, inane words. 'Think nothing of it,' she said airily. 'All in a day's work.'

Both Rory and Mike realised that she was trying to

lighten the moment now that all concerned were conscious of the need to act. Only Jonathan looked and sounded as bitter and resentful as before. He was staring at the floor, but now raised his eyes, dark with anger, and gave Kate a look so alien, so malevolent, that she instinctively moved her head backwards.

'*Et tu, Brute*?' he said, in bitter, low tones. The over-used phrase should have seemed theatrical, but it didn't. For once it fitted the situation perfectly. Kate felt a traitor. She was virtually stabbing him in the back by insisting on an open discussion, especially after leaving the restaurant so precipitately at lunchtime.

Jonathan would have left the room, but Mike barred his way.

'We've got to talk,' he said. 'Or rather arrange to talk, later, after surgery.'

'You fix it. You and my cousin, and my nearly fiancée. You fix it between you. I'll be there, I promise you that. I'll be there.'

He didn't even bang the door as he went, thought Kate inconsequentially. He's like a cornered animal. Appalled, she shied away from the thought.

She was aware that Mike and Rory were standing looking down at her. She was still sitting on the chair on to which she had collapsed when Rory had arrived a million years ago. She stood up. 'Well,' she said in her best nurse-manager voice, 'when and where are we going to hold this meeting?'

'It must be tonight, after surgery,' replied Mike, firm and determined now that he had got over the shock of seeing the Norths locked in a kind of mortal combat, and realised the gravity of the situation.

Kate asked Rory, 'Can you arrange something at the London end—I understand you had some sort of emergency?'

'I'll do my best,' he said, sounding and looking grim. 'May I use your phone? Might be more politic than going through to my——' he hesitated '——Uncle Matt's office.'

Mike looked from one to the other. He was still uneasy, but now determined to sort things out. 'Look,' he said. 'I think that you'd all better come to my place. Bella will see that we're not disturbed. That way, neither Matt, nor your mother, Kate, will be in any way involved.'

'That would be great.' For the first time in hours, Kate thought about her mother and poor Dora, upset and worried about her illness. 'Oh, my God!' she exclaimed. 'I must go home and see if they're all right.' She had forgotten that Mike wasn't in on the situation. He knew nothing of Dora's probable diabetes and the problems that would arise at Bathurst if she needed to be hospitalised.

Rory, of course, did know, and understood. 'You go home now, Kate,' he said gently, reverting to the kind, considerate man who had declared his love for her. 'I'll explain to Mike. I'm sure between us we'll work something out. And one of us will ring you to let you know about the meeting at Mike's home.'

'Are you sure?' she asked. 'Is it all right if I go?'

'Of course it's all right, love, off you go.' Rory pushed her gently through the door of her office. As if in a dream she collected her coat and handbag, locked the outer door, and made her way through Reception to the car park. Several people, patients and staff, called goodnight as she left, and like a zombie she responded.

'I must drive very carefully,' she reminded herself as she moved out of the car park, and realised as she said it that it was the second time that day that she'd driven with great care and concentration. She shrugged and gave a wry little smile as she turned out into the High Street. 'It's getting to be a habit,' she murmured as she headed for home.

CHAPTER TEN

KATE decided as she was driving home that she would try to put the problems relating to the health centre aside until she had sorted out how to cope with Dora's illness. She felt awful about having to go out that evening, but agreed with Mike that the situation had to be cleared up immediately. It would be a good thing to get what was likely to be a difficult session over and done with.

Before that she would have a chat with her mother and Dora about getting some extra help in the house, and arrange to have some days off herself. She had quite a backlog of holidays to catch up with, and only the events of the afternoon and Rory and Jonathan's behaviour had stopped her making arrangements there and then.

Ros Jacobs, her assistant, could manage for a week or so, as long as the problem with the doctors could be sorted out. 'And I'll damn well make sure that it is!' she muttered savagely as she turned into the drive.

Her anger with both the North men at least took the edge off her despair over her own feelings. It wouldn't last, she knew, but just at present she didn't care what happened to either Rory or Jonathan as long as the matter was resolved without harming the practice.

Whenever she thought of Rory, her stomach knotted up with longing and desire. She'd never felt this way about Jonathan, but then, he'd never kissed her the way Rory had, passionately, hurtfully, but at the same time lovingly. Jonathan's kisses had all been either perfunctory or hard and demanding, without love or tenderness, expressing need, desire but not compassion, and certainly not love.

She didn't know why this hadn't been clear before, or why it was now shiningly obvious. What wasted years, she thought. Can we ever make up for them? Will Jonathan ever forgive me for forcing him into a showdown with Rory and Mike? His bitterness when he had left her office made it unlikely. Yet, he was so prone to changing his mind, to wavering, to taking the line of least resistance that he might well decide to return to her as if nothing had happened.

She got out of the car and stood for a moment on the wide sweep of golden gravel in front of the coach-house. The storm had passed over, the orange sun had turned red and was fast sinking into rafts of pink-tinted, fluffy clouds. The sky overhead had the drained, washed look of a child's painting, too much water, not enough colour.

Across the drive the top half of the stable door leading to the kitchen stood open. She could hear Thomas's voice, rather shrill and excited as he chatted to Dora.

Thinking of Dora reminded Kate that she should get inside and help with supper. Surprisingly, it was not Dora, but her mother, up to her elbows in flour, who was sitting in her wheelchair at the long, low scrubbed table.

Thomas was emptying the dishwasher with exaggerated care, taking each plate and cup separately from the rack and placing each item on the dresser.

The scene was one of quiet domestic bliss, rather like a Dutch painting, dim and dark and lit only with the fading light from the setting sun.

Kate's heart missed a beat. 'Dora?' she asked breathlessly.

'Oh, hello, darling; look, Thomas and I are managing fine.' She realised how anxious Kate was. 'It's all right, love, I've sent Dora up to rest. She's tired, but otherwise OK.'

Thomas said proudly, 'Look, Kate, I'm emptying the machine. I'm being ever so careful.'

'So you are, darling.' Kate dropped a kiss on his head as she passed. She kissed her mother's cheek. 'Look, give me a minute and I'll take over here.' She made for the hall door.

'Why?' asked Mrs Christy. 'I'm enjoying myself. I don't often get a chance to do anything in Dora's kitchen, but she is tired and was quite happy to hand over to me for once. I am doing dumplings, by the way, for a stew which is almost ready. You go and change and be down in twenty minutes for supper.'

Kate stopped by the door. 'Are you sure?' she asked. 'Sure that you can manage?'

'Absolutely, especially with Thomas's help.'

Thomas shrilled out, chanting, 'I'm helping Granny, I'm helping Granny.'

'Yes,' said Kate with a grin. 'So I see.'

She had a quick shower and changed into jeans and a pink cashmere sweater. The phone rang just as she was about to leave her room. It was Mike. 'See you at my place at about eight,' he said.

When she went down to supper, Dora was already there, looking rather less strained than when Kate had last seen her in the surgery that morning.

She was clutching the diet sheet that Dr Lyons had given her. 'Follow that for a day or two,' the doctor had told her. 'Just till we find out exactly what is wrong. Better be on the safe side. Just go easy on the carbohydrates—that is starchy things—and cut out added sugar, cakes and biscuits.'

Dora was reading the diet suggestions out to Mrs Christy. When Kate came in, she asked anxiously, 'Will stew be all right for me to have for supper, and apple crumble for dessert?'

Before Kate could answer, Mrs Christy said sharply, 'Of course it will be all right, Dora, I've already told you. Only don't have any dumplings. It's only vegetable stew, it can't possibly hurt you.'

Dora looked at Kate. 'Is that right, Kate?' she asked.

Kate grinned and nodded. 'But I should skip the crumble, or just scoop out the fruit,' she suggested. She was used to the affectionate wrangling between the two women, though it was usually Dora who had the upper hand where food was concerned.

'Just what I said,' declared Mrs Christy triumphantly. 'I wasn't a GP's wife for nothing, you know. I learned a thing or two.'

'So you keep telling me,' retorted Dora, pretending to a huffiness that she didn't really feel.

Kate couldn't say much while they were having supper, though she would have liked to discuss possibilities for extra help while Dora was under the weather. Thomas was full of his doings at school and gave a blow-by-blow description of how he had performed in a game that seemed to be a mixture of rounders, football and cricket. Whatever it was, he appeared to have played a vital role in beating the opposition.

It was lovely to see him a happy, relaxed small boy instead of the guarded, truculent child of a few weeks ago. Had Rory North been so much of an influence on him? Was the change in Thomas mostly due to his interest?

Kate pushed the thought away. She didn't want to give Rory any Brownie points the way she felt about both him and Jonathan at present.

Dora left the table. 'I've got to go to the loo,' she said.

Kate said abruptly to her mother when Dora had left the room, 'I'm going to have a week or ten days off to help out while Dora's getting checked out. But it will take me a day or so to fix. I thought that I'd ask Dot Harrison if she'd come in and give a hand in the meanwhile. She's such a nice person, and I think that she'll be glad of the extra money. After that, we'll have to see what Dora's able to do. I don't think she's too bad, but she shouldn't work as hard as she has been doing.'

'I couldn't agree more,' said her mother forcefully. 'But don't you worry about it. I've already made arrangements for help in the house, and what's more Dora approves.'

Kate gaped. 'What do you mean, you've made arrangements?'

'Well, really, Kate, I mean exactly what I've said. Mona Makepiece happened to phone today, and guess what?'

'I'm beyond guessing,' replied Kate, trying to think what possible connection her mother's old schoolfriend could have with the current problem.

'Oona,' said Mrs Christy triumphantly. 'Mona's niece.'

'Isn't she in South America or somewhere in search of Inca artefacts or something?'

'She's just got back after a very successful trip and is preparing to go to India or Tibet, or somewhere like that. Anyway, she wants a job for a few months while she's getting sponsorship and putting together an expedition.'

Oona Makepiece, thought Kate, only a couple of years older than I am, yet she's been all over the world while I've been mouldering away in Midchester. Hell, I wish I could do the same!

That wasn't true, of course. She could never, and in her heart knew that she wouldn't want to, emulate Oona, who breezed in every few years to see them. She was always going to or coming back from some distant location but had said on more than one occasion that she envied Kate.

Kate had hooted with laughter. 'Envy me? My goodness, you don't know what you're talking about.'

'Oh, yes, I do,' Oona had said, looking wistfully round the comfortable kitchen. 'I mean all this, and your lovely, loving mother.'

And Oona wasn't selfish either. She hadn't any family except for her Aunt Mona, Mrs Christy's old schoolfriend. Mona always made her welcome, kept a room ready for her, but couldn't offer more. She was a bridge-playing socialite with a circle of similar friends, who had nothing in common with her adventurous niece.

'When's Oona coming?' Kate asked, still amazed by the speed with which her mother had made arrangements for help.

'Tomorrow evening; she's got some radio and television interviews to do before then. But after that she'll be free for a couple of months while she's preparing for her next trip. Isn't it great? She's such a lovely, cheerful girl, and so very practical, in spite of her looks. She'll come and help out here, if I help sponsor her for wherever it is that she's going next.'

Oona's looks were one of the things that made her the darling of TV interviewers. Most men came over all protective and totally chauvinistic when they first met her, looking tiny, frail and in need of macho support. If they did but know her! Kate had often thought. She was as tough as old boots, had a frightful temper when roused, though this was rare and usually for good reason, and could give anyone as good as she got. She was a splendid horsewoman, fast driver and a competent pilot.

Of course those who interviewed her knew this, but found it hard to believe. They made a great thing about

her daintiness, her pretty clothes, the expensive perfume that she supposedly had a passion for, and always
they tried to link her name with a newsworthy candi-
date. No way did they want to accept her toughness
and self-sufficiency. She must need, or at least want a
man.

Arriving a little late at the Dollands', Kate found Mike,
Jonathan and Rory glued to the TV in Mike's study,
watching Oona being interviewed in a news round-up.

'What an absolute cracker!' Mike was saying as she
entered.

'Gorgeous girl, and bright with it,' agreed Rory.

'I met her once,' announced Jonathan, to his com-
panions' surprise.

'Met her?' they said in unison.

'Yes,' said Kate from just inside the door. 'At
Bathurst. My mother is an old schoolfriend of her
aunt.'

The three men, whom Kate had expected to find, if
not at daggers drawn, at least on the defensive with
each other, seemed on quite good terms. It only takes
an exceptionally pretty girl to distract them, she
thought irritably.

They all looked a bit embarrassed. Mike came
forward to greet her. 'Kate, come and sit down. What'll
you have to drink?'

'A dry Martini, please.'

Rory switched off the set. 'Sorry about that,' he said,
though he didn't sound particularly sorry. His eyes lit
up when he looked at her. 'Is everything all right at
home?'

'Of course, why shouldn't it be? And with Oona
Makepiece coming tomorrow to look after everything,
it couldn't be better.' She had deliberately dropped a
bombshell.

'Do you mean. . .?' Mike gestured towards the blank

television screen. He made an effort to pull himself together. 'Do you mean that Oona Makepiece is going to stay at your house?'

'Yes.'

'Gosh!' he exclaimed in his slightly old-fashioned manner. 'How marvellous. And when you say that she's coming to look after things, do you mean. . .?' He dried up, at a loss for words.

Kate took pity on him. 'Oona is going to look after my mother, Thomas and Dora, and help run things for a few weeks until we get things sorted out. She's very competent, you know, and not nearly as fragile as she looks.' She put on her professional voice and manner. 'Now, are we going to discuss the practice? After all, that's what we're here for, isn't it?' She couldn't keep a hint of sarcasm out of her voice. 'Or are you desperate to see more of the delectable Oona?'

What was it, she wondered, that affected all men, even those as sophisticated and assured as Rory, when a really stunning girl appeared, that turned them into gaping idiots? She wondered how they would react when they met Oona in the flesh. Without any feeling of jealousy, she looked forward to the occasion.

Mike cleared his throat. 'Kate, we seem to have got over the worst since this afternoon. Matt has been in touch. He guessed that we might be having some sort of get-together to sort things out. Jonathan has the details.'

Jonathan had lost both his decisiveness and bitterness, but he said in a fairly firm voice, 'Dad will make an official announcement about leaving the practice in the next week or so. Meanwhile he asks that we keep things going as they are at present.'

'You mean that nothing's really changed at all?' asked Kate, anger stirring in her again. Had he really put her through all this anguish for nothing? Had she turned down Rory in order to be seen to support

Jonathan, for nothing? She felt the blood rushing to her face and her hands trembling. Through clenched teeth, she said, 'Tell me, honestly if you can, Jonathan, was there any point in our celebratory lunch today? Had your father really said that he was going to retire?'

Rory got up from the deep armchair in which he had been sitting. 'Kate,' he said softly, moving to where she was sitting. He put a hand on her shoulder.

His touch was electrifying, his nearness made her tremble more than ever. Miraculously, neither Mike, nor, more importantly, Jonathan, seemed to notice. She knew that she should try again to shake off his hand, but couldn't. She was raging inside, furious with him for making her feel helpless.

He crouched before her, compelling her to look into his eyes. Those sea-green eyes, flecked with gold when he was in a kind or tender mood, as now. Her insides melted as she read the message of love in those gold-green eyes. She was limp and breathless with longing, her pulse pounded in her ears, she felt dizzy, other sounds in the room faded away, the blood drained from her face.

She thought with surprise, I'm going to faint, but I never faint. Rory had his hand on the back of her neck and was pushing her head down between her knees. He said something and Mike and Jonathan were suddenly standing there, all three of them were speaking. Their voices came and went on waves of sound. There was a sharp smell in her nostrils. Ammonia. The pounding in her ears began to subside, the blood came back into her face. She felt better.

Bella's voice, light and insubstantial against the chorus of deep male voices, broke through her wavering senses. Kate opened her eyes. Bella was kneeling at her feet wafting a bottle of smelling-salts beneath her nose.

Kate sat up carefully—her head still felt as if it didn't

belong to her. 'Oh, how incredibly stupid of me. I just don't believe it. . .' she said, smiling at Bella and then at Mike. Jonathan and Rory. She looked at the bottle in Bella's hand. 'Thanks,' she added.

'Think nothing of it,' grinned Bella. 'Simple first aid, which these idiots seem to have forgotten. Talk about panic!' The three men looked sheepish.

'Well, I would have got something from my case,' said Mike. 'It just seemed quicker to ask for your smelling-salts.' He grinned back at his wife. Kate thought how well they understood each other.

Jonathan knelt down beside her chair. 'Kate, darling, how do you feel now?' he asked, his eyes anxious, concerned.

'I'm fine, I don't know what on earth made me faint. I've *never* fainted before. It must be this thundery heat or something.' She put a hand up to the high neck of her sweater and eased it away from her skin.

The three men shifted uncomfortably. Heat or no heat, they all felt somewhat responsible for Kate's state of mind and body. They'd each put pressure on her during the day one way or the other. Even Mike, less involved than the other two, had needed her to remind him of his responsibilities and prod him into action.

Bella said, with a laugh in her voice, 'Perhaps you should see a doctor. I hear there's quite a good one in the practice across the river.'

Kate smiled; she was grateful for Bella's sense of humour. 'I'll bear that in mind,' she said. 'Now I think I'd better get off home before I disgrace myself further.'

'I'll drive you back,' offered Jonathan at once. 'If I may leave my car here, Mike, and pick it up in the morning?'

'Of course.'

Rory, standing behind, but head and shoulders above the others, said, 'I'd better push off now, back to town.' He smiled round at everyone. 'So pleased everything's sorted out. See you all on Friday. Thanks for the hospitality, Mike, Bella.' He shook hands and turned to his cousin. 'Goodnight, Jonathan.' He shook him by the hand too, and turned to Kate. 'Glad you don't make a habit of passing out.' He smiled a smile that she knew was just for her, although it must have looked quite ordinary to the others. 'Much too alarming for three unprepared medicos.' He gripped her hand and left.

Mike went out to see him off. Kate heard the Lotus move away down the drive. She didn't know how she was going to survive till the end of the week.

CHAPTER ELEVEN

IN FACT, the few days between Rory's departure and his return passed in a flash.

Oona arrived at Bathurst to a rapturous welcome from Mrs Christy, Dora, and, after some initial reservations, Thomas. When prompted, he vaguely remembered Oona from a visit some two years earlier, when she had presented him with a much loved, now rather tatty, woolly African elephant. This time she brought him a companion soft toy in the shape of a giant anteater from South America.

Thomas instantly named the thick, furry creature with a long snout and bushy tail, looking incredibly lifelike—Snooty. He was enchanted with his present and with Oona, who, Kate observed, immediately established a bond with her nephew.

The day after her arrival, Oona asked, 'Who is Rory?' and added, 'Thomas is full of him and his doings.'

'He's Dr Matt North's nephew and has come to help out while Dr North is recovering from his heart condition,' Kate explained, her own heart thudding uncomfortably at the very mention of Rory, and the vaguest sense of foreboding that somehow Oona's presence would effect their gossamer-thin relationship.

But Oona was only mildly interested in this information. She was much more interested to hear of Dr Matt North.

'Oh, that nice old doctor who is chatting up your Mum,' she replied. 'He called in. He's a sweetie and obviously thinks Mrs Christy is the tops. He's really dead keen on her, isn't he? They make a smashing pair. By the way, didn't I meet another handsome North who was pursuing you like mad when I was last here. Is he still around?'

'Yes, he's still around.'

'Still in hot pursuit?' asked Oona with a nice smile that took any impertinence out of the question.

'You could say that,' agreed Kate. For one wild moment she thought of confiding her muddled thoughts to this bright, intelligent young woman, but the moment passed. To voice her reservations about Jonathan smacked of disloyalty.

Oona's remarks about her mother and Dr North senior jolted her considerably. For, although she had noticed their increasing interest in each other, she had not realised that it was apparent to anyone else. Nor had she thought it significant until Oona had suggested it.

The idea that Matt North and her mother might have a serious and mutual interest in each other was disconcerting. It added yet another dimension to the problem of breaking away from Jonathan. For she had decided, over the past days, that, whatever the outcome of her growing relationship with Rory, she must be honest with Jonathan and tell him that anything more than friendship between them, was now out of the question.

Perhaps some of Oona's extrovert courage and forthrightness had rubbed off on her. Oona's attitude had always been, 'Go out and get it.' Kate knew that Oona would never willingly hurt anybody, but if she wanted something enough she would grab every opportunity to obtain it. And perhaps her more straightforward way was kinder all round.

Well, ultimately, what she herself was proposing to do to Jonathan would benefit him. The picture had clarified. Marrying him just because she felt motherly and concerned for him was not enough; it wouldn't be fair to either of them.

With an honesty that she had not previously adopted, Kate considered dispassionately her relationship with Jonathan North. She had been prepared to accept his vacillations and childish determination to get his own way because she loved him and thought her love returned. Now she could see that the love he had for her was mostly inspired by his need for someone strong to direct and support him.

Well, she was no longer prepared to go on offering this maternal-type of support. She too sometimes needed someone to lean on, to utterly depend upon. No longer would she be a crutch to Jonathan.

On the third day of Rory's absence, Dora was admitted to the Cottage Hospital for further investigations and stabilisation of future medication and diet. She was indeed suffering from diabetes, but in a fairly mild form that should be easy to control.

Kate took her into hospital and saw her safely installed. 'I'll come back this evening to visit,' she promised, knowing that, behind the brave face, Dora was very anxious. 'You'll be all right, darling, I promise. The staff here are lovely.'

She arranged the flowers that her mother had picked with loving care just before they left. 'Oh, look, one of Mummy's orchids from the hot house. You are honoured.' She gave the snow-white blooms cascading down a thread-like stem pride of place in front of the vase.

With relief, Kate heard Dora giggle. Their eyes met over the loaded vase. 'Do you think that she's trying to tell me something?' Dora asked. 'Like I'm going to miss you, especially in the kitchen?'

Kate laughed with her. In spite of her mother's pretending to be pleased to do some cooking the other night, both she and Dora knew that it wasn't her forte. They also knew that she hated picking her orchids, and

to have done so on this occasion was an indication of
her love and affection for her old friend.

'She'll miss me when I'm gone,' stated Dora, still
chuckling.

'Won't we all?' said Kate with a smile, bending to
give the older lady a kiss. 'Not,' she added hastily,
'that your demise is imminent. Not with a tough old
bird like you.'

'Do you mind?' said Dora, pretending to be huffy.
'Not so much of the old!'

Kate worked late on Thursday evening. She was putting everything in order to take a week's leave, starting
from Friday lunchtime. She longed to see Rory, but
some perverse streak made her arrange to be away
from the centre from the time he was due back.

There was a knock at her door and it opened before
she had time to answer .

'Hello,' said Rory. 'I thought I'd find you here.'

Kate was struck dumb with surprise.

'You didn't expect to see me now,' stated Rory in a
matter-of-fact voice.

Kate stared at him, and mumbled, 'No, I thought
that you weren't coming back till tomorrow.'

'So did I, Kate, so did I. But the fates were on our
side; my last patient, due to be seen tonight, cancelled
and I decided not to waste time, to get back as soon as
possible. We have to talk, Kate.'

'Oh.' She looked at his dark charcoal-grey suit, pale-
grey shirt and university tie, and said inconsequentially,
'Yes, I see that you have come straight from work.'

'Hot-footed, as they say.'

'Rory. . .'

'Kate. . .?'

'I'm so muddled. I don't know what to say.' She
slumped over her desk. Everything seemed futile.

'What does anything matter?' she muttered tonelessly. 'I don't know how to go on. It all seems so pointless.'

'Oh, come on, Kate, not a bit pointless. You know that really. Everyone needs you. The practice needs you, Jonathan needs you.' He crossed the room and put his arms round her, pulling her up from the chair as he did so. 'Kate,' he whispered in her ear, '*I* need you. Be brave, my dear, carry on and do what you must. Matters will resolve themselves in due course.'

He held her close. It was the embrace of a loving friend, not that of a lover. She leaned against his broad chest, feeling safe and secure. He kissed the top of her head with infinite gentleness and blew softly at the fine strands of hair on her forehead. The solidity of him was a supreme comfort. She could have stayed folded in his arms forever.

The phone rang. It was Rachel, the last doctor that evening on duty. 'Kate, come at once, please. Bring the oxygen. I've got a patient here in respiratory difficulties.'

Rory heard what she said, and, without a word, collected the cylinder from the clinic-room, as Kate picked up the resuscitation tray.

'A bronchitic and asthma attack combined,' said Rachel, not taking her eyes off her patient as they entered her office.

She was bending over an elderly man sitting slumped in a chair with his head and shoulders hunched over the back of a second chair. His breathing was loud and stertorous, coming in great, heaving inspirations and difficult, jerky exhalations. There was a bluish tinge round his mouth, and, Kate found when she touched him, he was cold and clammy.

'May I?' asked Rory of Rachel, kneeling down beside her and in front of the patient.

'Rory, am I glad that you're here!' Obviously Rachel hadn't realised that he was there until this moment.

'Kate, let's have a mask and the oxygen stat,' Rory said briskly, and then spoke quietly to the patient whom he recognised. 'It's OK, Mr Spooner, we'll soon have you feeling more comfortable.' He placed the mask that Kate had handed to him gently over the old man's nose. 'There, now, slowly does it. Long, steady breaths if you can manage it.' He nodded at Kate. 'Low volume,' he said softly, 'mustn't aggravate his exhalations.'

Every so often he lifted the mask away from the patient's face, which was gradually returning to something like normal from the putty colour it had presented when they had first arrived on the scene. The blue circle round his mouth had disappeared. 'Carry on with the oxygen, Kate, for another couple of minutes, while Rachel decides what should be done next.'

'A courteous man,' Mrs Christy had called him, Kate recalled as she took over from him, and how right she was. With all his experience and qualifications, he had no intention of upstaging young Dr Lyons. Mr Spooner was her patient, and it would be she who would determine what follow-up treatment the old man would have.

She heard them murmuring about various respiratory stimulants and aids, and wondered which one Rachel would plump for.

'Aminophylline,' decided Rachel. 'By injection now and choledyl for him to take at home by mouth.' She was definite about her choice of medication, but added a little uncertainly, 'Do you think that Mr Spooner should go into hospital for assessment?' She looked at Rory, wanting his advice, but cross with herself for having to ask for it.

'A sensible precaution,' he replied, giving her a nice friendly smile. 'No rush, now that you've sorted out his immediate problem, just a routine admission so that he can have tests and daily checks.'

Rachel flushed with pleasure at his implied satisfaction with her intended treatment.

'Shall I draw up the injection, Doctor?' Kate asked, feeling the need to be formal.

Rachel seemed for a moment surprised to find her there. 'Oh, please, Sister, and will you give it? You're marvellous with injections.' She gave Kate a radiant smile. 'Thanks,' she added.

'My pleasure,' said Kate, hiding her surprise at the doctor's open praise.

'I'll take Mr Spooner home,' offered Rory. 'He doesn't want to hang around waiting for a bus.'

'Oh, I could manage, sir,' said Mr Spooner, still wheezy, though looking much improved. 'The bus won't be long a-coming.'

'It's on my way, Mr Spooner,' said Rory in a casual manner. 'I might as well drop you off.'

A few minutes later Rory, giving the old man his arm for support, left the centre. 'I'll phone,' he said softly to Kate. 'Don't make any arrangements for tomorrow till we've had a word.'

Rachel was grateful and full of praise for both Kate and Rory. 'I still panic a bit when an emergency occurs and I haven't the usual hospital back-up. You were both great, and not a bit pushy.' She sighed. 'Isn't Rory wonderful? Amazing he isn't married or anything.'

'Amazing,' confirmed Kate.

The small emergency had given her the necessary rush of adrenalin to enable her to pull herself together. She was grateful too for the respite that the unexpected call for help had given her, interrupting, as it had, her reunion with Rory. For all the comfort and strength which his presence had provided, she longed for time in which to come to terms with the new direction that life seemed to be taking.

She said goodnight to Rachel and drove home

through the gathering dusk, calling in at the Cottage Hospital on the way to see Dora as promised. She only stayed a few minutes, as Dora was sitting in the day-room with another lady with whom she had obviously connected. They were immersed in a television programme.

In the driveway of Bathurst stood two cars, the rather battered estate belonging to Mike Dolland, and Jonathan's smart new Suzuki Swift 1.6 GLX, a birthday present from his father.

The top half of the stable door of the kitchen stood open to the still, balmy air of the night. A stream of golden light streaked across the gravel, and the sound of laughter and cheerfully raised voices greeted Kate as she crossed the drive.

In the kitchen she found Mike, Jonathan, her mother, Thomas in his pyjamas, and Oona, a tea-towel round her waist, dishing up something aromatic from the top of the Aga.

Kate stood for a moment unobserved, watching everyone watching Oona. 'The Jungle Girl,' as one paper had nicknamed her, was like a magnet, drawing the eyes not only of the two mature men present, but riveting the attention of Mrs Christy and young Thomas as well.

She's certainly a special kind of person, thought Kate without jealousy or rancour. There was something about Oona that made her as likeable to her own sex as to the typical male chauvinist.

'Hi, everybody,' said Kate, leaning on the half-door. Thomas and Oona returned her greeting. 'Hi,' they said in unison. Mrs Christy said, 'Hello, darling, just in time for Oona's Tamale pie, a Mexican speciality.' The two men half rose to their feet. They looked faintly uncomfortable, as if they were playing truant.

Oona said, 'Come and sit down, old thing, and have a drink. Jonathan, fill up a glass for Kate.'

Kate sat down at the kitchen table, glad to be home and grateful to Oona for being there and organising the evening meal and seeing to Thomas. She began to relax.

'Smells delicious,' she commented, as Oona placed a steaming plate covered in golden pastry before her. 'What's in it?'

'Minced meat, olives, peppers and so on. I've reduced the amount of chilli powder on account of sir here.' Oona ruffled Thomas's hair. 'Should use maize flour, but I couldn't get hold of that, so I had to make the pastry with stone-ground wholemeal. But it should be OK.'

It was more than okay—it was a 'culinary experience', as both Mike and Jonathan remarked several times. Mrs Christy and Kate exchanged secret, smiling glances as the two men grew more vocal in their praise of the meal. It was quite clear that they were both besotted with Oona.

Mike, however, got up to leave as soon as supper was over. 'Bella's going to ring at about nine,' he said. 'She's gone to see her mother, who isn't well, and is going to stay the night. She suggested that I came here with my begging-bowl to be fed, as she had to rush off in a hurry.'

Clever Bella, thought Kate, making sure that he had a chance to meet Oona without feeling guilty. 'I'll see you out,' she said, and walked to the garage with him.

Mike grinned at her in the glimmering half-twilight of stars and lamplight. 'I've got a clever and beautiful wife, Kate. We understand each other. My head's tilted but not turned by the delectable Oona.'

'Exactly what I would expect, Mike,' Kate replied quietly. 'You've a marriage to be envied.'

'Yep, I guess we have, but you have to start off with the right person and work at it.' Mike got into his car and leaned out of the window. 'Don't make a mistake and choose the wrong person, Kate. Goodnight.' He took off with a spurt of gravel.

Oh, I won't, she thought as she returned to the kitchen. Rather nobody than the wrong man.

Thomas was waiting to be put to bed when she returned. How like Oona not to usurp me completely, thought Kate, shooing her nephew up the stairs and listening with half an ear to his excited chatter. 'I like her,' he said as she tucked him into bed. 'Almost as much as Rory.'

'My feelings exactly,' replied Kate, giving him a kiss and tucking the African elephant and the South American ant-eater in beside him. 'Goodnight, love, God bless.'

Kate was able to leave the medical centre just after eleven on Friday morning. She had dealt with the few bloods and other specimens requiring investigation at the hospital laboratory. As usual, the doctors had only asked for urgent cases to be investigated prior to the weekend.

It seemed rather strange to her that both Rory and Dr North senior had phoned her during the morning. Rory wanted to know if she would go out with him that evening. 'For a quiet meal somewhere,' he'd suggested, 'where we can talk, as well as eat.'

Against her will, though longing to see him, she had agreed. 'Great,' he said. 'It's a bit of a Cinderella-like situation, as I'm on call from midnight.'

Trying to sound cool and sophisticated, Kate had replied that that suited her.

'Right,' said Rory. 'I'll collect you at seven. Be ready.' He had sounded brisk and almost calculating. If he hadn't put down the phone she would probably have argued with him.

Dr Matt North had asked her to visit him. 'Preferably while Jonathan's out on calls,' he'd suggested. Bearing in mind Oona's comments, Kate presumed that the doctor wanted to say something about his friendship with her mother. A role reversal, she thought, suppressing a giggle, the oldies putting forward their case for seeing each other.

Kate left the centre at half-past eleven, happy to be free of nursing responsibilities until Monday week. In spite of all her problems and some reservations about her meeting with Dr Matt North, she felt more relaxed than she had for days.

Dora, given the right treatment, was going to be almost as fit as usual. Mrs Christy and Oona were going to visit her this afternoon, leaving Kate free to prepare for once in a leisurely fashion for an evening out. Jonathan had been invited weeks ago to an old-boys' reunion at his school in Dorset, and was leaving early in the afternoon, so there were no difficult explanations to make to him.

If the fates, as Rory had said, had made it possible for him to get back to Midchester earlier, they had also cleared the way for Kate to go out without feeling guilty. Jonathan had been unusually cheerful when he'd come on duty that morning, and he seemed to be looking forward to his visit to his old school.

Dr North was on the terrace as he had been when Kate made a previous visit. But this time he was able to get up to greet her and offer her a chair. He looked much better, almost his old self.

'I'm having a pre-lunch sherry, Kate; will you join me, or would you prefer coffee?'

'The sherry would be lovely, as long as I can have a biscuit or two to mop up any excess alcohol before I drive. I've just started my holiday, so I feel entitled to a drink.'

'Good.' The doctor poured her drink with great care into the plain crystal glass. It was a fine dry light wine that he knew she liked. He held it up to the muted autumn sunlight before he handed it to her, and they both admired the pale golden liquid filling the glass almost to the brim.

Kate took a sip and nodded her appreciation.

Dr North said, 'I won't preamble, Kate. I want to talk to you about Jonathan and Rory.'

She was so surprised that she spilt some sherry. 'Jonathan and Rory?' she repeated stupidly.

'Just so.'

'Well, what about them? They're getting on reasonably well at present. What with Rory only being around at the weekend, and your message about carrying on as usual till you make your announcement about retiring, the tension has lessened.'

'I don't know if you are being deliberately obtuse, Kate, but I meant my son and my nephew in relation to you. That's what I want to talk about.'

Her first reaction was to say that it had nothing whatsoever to do with him. As she was a mature woman, he had no right to pry into her affairs, even if they happened to be connected with his son and his nephew. But old loyalties, old morals and manners instilled by her mother made her pause. She had known Dr Matt North since she was a small girl. Her mother had never made any secret about the fact that she admired and respected the older doctor, and that she was sometimes guided by him. These same considerations now made Kate think before she spoke.

When she did, it was to ask politely just what he meant. Just as politely, Dr North replied, 'You've been good to my boy, Kate, and I've been grateful for your goodness, but the time has come to be honest. I know that you don't love him——' he hesitated '—no, I don't mean that, I mean that you are not *in* love with him. Never have been. Consciously or not, you've let love of a maternal sort influence the way you feel about him.'

Kate gasped with surprise at the aptness of Dr North's remarks. Just what she'd been thinking a short while before.

The old doctor seemed not to have noticed her reaction. 'What I'm asking you to do, Kate, is release him. He will never have the strength to do it. You must.'

'That's not very fair,' she said, though privately acknowledging that this was precisely what she had intended.

'No, I'm afraid that the strong always have to assume responsibility for the weak.'

After a moment and another sip at her drink, she asked, 'And Rory, what did you want to tell me about Rory?'

'Only that he was in no way responsible for what happened twenty years ago. He left to spare me further distress. He hadn't stolen anything. The business about the missing jewels was just a figment of my late wife's imagination. She hid the jewels—I found them and a note when she died. She always saw Rory as a threat to Jonathan, Rory being the son of the eldest son of the family, due to inherit the title when his father died. I think she imagined in her muddled fashion that making him out to be a thief would change everything.'

'I see.' But Kate didn't really. It was such a bizarre thing to have happened. 'Title,' she asked, 'what title?' At least she could get that straight.

'Sir,' said Dr North. 'The eldest son inherits the title of a baronet. My brother was the eldest son—Rory's entitled to it, but seldom uses it.' He didn't seem surprised that she didn't know anything about it.

So Jonathan had been speaking the truth when he referred to his cousin as 'Sir'. It hadn't been a piece of sarcasm, as she had thought. What else, she wondered as she drove home, was the distinguished Sir Rowland North hiding? His reasons for not divulging his title might be sound, noble even, but she felt deceived. It was as if she would be meeting a stranger that night. A man even more enigmatic than she had imagined.

Rory collected her as arranged. They drove a long way out of town along the riverside, making easy, desultory conversation about nothing in particular. Eventually they reached a barge converted into a restaurant, moored in an isolated backwater. It was almost full when they arrived, and Kate wondered how it attracted so much trade, as it was so out of the way.

They were shown to a table tucked away into a tiny curtained alcove. It was made for the quiet, intimate dinner that he had suggested. 'Owned by an ex-patient of mine, though he's away at the moment,' Rory explained. 'Has a word-of-mouth reputation for good food and service.'

And wildly expensive, guessed Kate. She leafed through the booklet-type menu, a plain print affair, unpriced! The opposite to the flamboyant tabloid-size menus she'd seen in some places.

She looked up and saw Rory watching her over the top of his menu. His eyes were glinting green and gold and full of merriment and admiration.

'I haven't told you how marvellous you look in that outfit,' he said. 'Or how delicious you smell, all country-fresh and wholesome.'

She wasn't quite sure about the wholesome; it sounded rather sturdy and plain. Rory sensed her reservation. 'My darling, I mean that as a unique compliment,' he assured her. 'I've never said that to anyone before.'

Not meaning to be acid, but sounding it, she answered, 'Well, I'm sure you've had plenty of practice dishing out the compliments to poor, unsuspecting females, *Sir* Rowland.' The minute the words were out she wished that she might retract them.

He looked not so much surprised by her comment as sad. The twinkle left his eyes and so did the golden highlights, leaving them sea-green and cold.

'Ah,' he said softly, 'you've heard about that; I was going to explain if you didn't already know.'

'Really?'

'Yes, really, Kate. Come on, my dear, don't hold that against me. It's an accident of birth, nothing more. I simply assumed that you knew; that's why I haven't mentioned it before. Your mother's such a good friend of Uncle Matt's. She must have known about the title.'

For the moment Kate was off balance. Yes, her mother must have known about it. Why hadn't she said anything? Perhaps, said a small voice inside her head, because she realised that it was not unduly important. So why am I making such a thing of it? she asked herself. Because it's all part of the secrecy, the uncertainty that has surrounded Rory ever since I first heard about him from Jonathan.

She lowered her eyes; she couldn't meet those clear, cold ones opposite. 'I'm sorry,' she mumbled, 'very sorry—it just came as such a surprise when your uncle told me this morning.'

'What else did he tell you, Kate?'

'The reason why you went away years ago. But, Rory, I never did think that you were a——'

'Thief?'

She nodded.

'Good,' he said briskly. 'I'm glad that you were able to accept me as an honest, if tarnished, broker.' He sounded terribly bitter or hurt, or both. 'Look, my dear, let's have a decent meal and try to enjoy it. I don't think that I can say all that I wanted to say to you now. The moment, dear girl, is spoilt.'

She made a negative gesture with her hand. 'No, that's not true, surely?'

'Yes, it is, Kate, but perhaps it's just as well. I know

that you're not ready for decision-making yet, and, though I was sure about it at the time, perhaps even I, in spite of my advanced years——' he gave a quirky smile '—was rushing my fences. I'm taking up a new post in the New Year. It takes time to consolidate before taking on more commitments.' He lowered his eyes and became absorbed in the menu.

Kate sat feeling as if she were turned to stone. Only her poor, tired mind seemed to be functioning, as she went over and over what he had said. So, it seemed, he had changed his mind about her anyway. This was the brush-off. It had nothing to do with her sarcasm over his title, or with the conversation that she'd had with his uncle earlier in the day.

He had already planned to tell her that he wasn't really in love with her, or, if he was, he could wait. Had she not made her ill-timed remarks, forcing him to speak before he was ready, he would have couched his rejection in clever, erudite phrases over their intimate dinner. But it would have been a rejection, none the less.

It just goes to show, she admitted to herself wearily, that the North men—well, her generation at least— were unreliable. A conclusion she'd reached once before, she recalled.

Pride and anger made her sit out the dinner, making stilted, idle conversation and pretending to enjoy the meal. She hoped that the delicious and unusual dishes she chose would cost him a bomb. She hoped that having to spend money on a lost cause would hurt him. It probably wouldn't, she mused, since he was well heeled, but perhaps his pride, like hers, would be hurt if she could stick out the evening.

She prayed for the ill-starred intimate occasion to be over, and at last it was. They drove home in silence beneath the stars and the moonlight and everything that nature could throw at them to make it a romantic affair.

Only when they stopped on the gravel sweep in front of the garage at Bathurst did Rory discard, to some degree, his lofty, arrogant pose. He turned to Kate, took her hands in his, and murmured softly, 'It shouldn't have been like this, my dear, dear love. Please remember, I'l always be around if you want me. You've only to call and I'll come running.'

Her heart felt like lead. She couldn't respond to his extravagant words, even if she had wanted to. All she wanted was to get to her room before she made a fool of herself and begged him to give her any scraps of affection that he might have left over after he'd met his medical commitments.

'Goodnight; thanks for my dinner,' she squeezed out between tight lips, before leaping from the car and rushing up to her room.

CHAPTER TWELVE

OCTOBER passed and suddenly it was November. A bleak foggy month which Kate felt exactly matched her bleakness of spirit.

Rory still came down on Thursday or Friday of each week but he and Kate avoided each other like the plague. If they met accidentally they were icily polite. It was a totally unreal situation that they hated but couldn't seem to remedy. Behaving in this childish fashion was alien to them both. But each believed the other out of love and too entangled with other issues to give way to their instincts.

Only the slow convalescence of Dr Matt North kept Rory around, and the fact that Jonathan, once so fiercely opposed to his presence, asked him to continue helping out.

Old Dr North had not yet made his announcement about retiring. 'Like the birth of a Royal baby,' said Mike sardonically. 'It's imminent but not yet ready to greet its public.'

Kate went through each day like an automaton. All joy had gone out of life for her since her parting with Rory following the disastrous dinner they'd shared.

She knew that some time soon she would have to make positive plans for the future. A future not associated with Midchester or the medical centre. Perhaps, her gloomy thoughts occasionally suggested, she would give up nursing altogether. For the first time ever in her life she considered a career other than nursing. For the first time in her life the daily chores associated with her chosen profession failed to absorb her. To her horror, she became a clock-watcher.

She fulfilled her duty periods competently, but couldn't wait for each session in the centre or domiciliary visits to be over. The irony was that when she got home, tired and dispirited, she found no relief—she might just as well have remained on duty. In fact, pretending in front of her mother, Dora and Oona was exhausting. It was easier to deceive Thomas, though he occasionally asked why Rory hadn't called. He seemed unaware of any change in her, but his chatter was tiring and she quickly grew irritated. A condition which in turn generated a feeling of guilt.

If the days were an agony of leaden despair to get through, the nights were infinitely worse. She lay awake for hour after hour trying to come to terms with her hopeless love for Rory, longing to feel his hands caressing her and his lips fastened on hers with the passion he had once displayed. It began to show. Unaware of how thin and lack-lustre she had become over the last few weeks, Kate continued to greet her colleagues and patients with a forced cheerfulness that she thought concealed her true state of mind.

Most of the staff and all the patients were unaware of her feelings for Rory. Those who thought themselves in the know assumed that her despair was due to Jonathan's barely disguised infatuation with Oona.

Mike suggested to Jonathan that he should speak to Kate, persuade her to take some time off, perhaps go away somewhere. Jonathan, who had been avoiding a tête-à-tête with Kate because he was reluctant to tell her about himself and Oona, was evasive.

'Well, if not you, perhaps your father would have a word? Believe me, Jonathan, our once calm and capable Sister Christy is heading for a breakdown.'

Mike wouldn't have been so sure, but Bella had put him in the picture about the abortive situation existing between Rory and Kate.

'But how do you know?' he'd asked in a bewildered

voice when his wife had first broached the subject. 'No one's said anything to me. Are you sure?'

'Positive, believe me.'

Mike did. He had great respect for Bella's intuition and intelligence. If she thought that something was amiss between Rory and Kate, then it was, no doubt about it.

Jonathan capitulated. 'OK,' he said. 'I'll have a word.'

Before he could do so, however, Rory arrived back one Friday rather earlier than usual and ran into Kate in the corridor. He was shocked by her appearance, and said so.

'What do you mean,' said Kate belligerently, trying to pass him in the narrow passageway and wondering why he had broken their rules of engagement, 'looking like a ghost?'

'Because, my dear girl, that's exactly how you look.'

Kate stared suspiciously at him in the dimmish light, and gave a harsh laugh. 'You don't look so brilliant yourself,' she retorted, wanting to put a hand up to his lined cheeks and shadowed eyes. Instead, she drew away from him as if he were infectious. 'And,' she added fiercely, 'I am not your "dear girl", never have been and never will be. And, for good measure, let me tell you that I'm just about to take a week off if Jonathan agrees.' She was proud of the idea suddenly springing to mind.

Briefly Rory looked pole-axed. 'Good,' he said softly, after a moment. 'You look as if you could do with a good rest.'

Kate stared at him angrily and tried to think of a smart retort but couldn't. She snorted miserably, holding back the tears that threatened because of his physical closeness and the psychological distance that she was convinced lay between them.

'Will you let me pass, please?' she asked in the coldest voice she could muster.

Without another word, Rory stood to one side. Kate went straight to Jonathan's office. There was a patient with him, but she asked if she might have a word when the patient left. She mooned up and down the corridor until Mrs Brown, slowly hobbling with two sticks, left.

'Sorry to keep you, Sister,' said the lady apologetically, seeing Kate hovering.

Kate was full of compunction. 'Oh, please don't worry about me, Mrs Brown. I'm not in any hurry. How's the arthritis, any improvement with the new tablets?'

'Oh, yes, I'm much better, thank you, and the physio helps that Dr Rory North started me on. He's a card, that one.'

'Yes,' agreed Kate tonelessly. 'He's certainly a card.' Adding to herself, he's a real Joker.

Jonathan, relieved that he didn't have to seek her out and propose a holiday, couldn't have been more amiable. 'Go off, dear Kate, at once,' he said. 'Go away somewhere and try to relax.'

In spite of her misery, Kate managed a faint smile. 'Pleased to get rid of me, Jonathan—leaving you a clear field with——?'

The telephone shrilled urgently. How often, she thought, as he picked up the receiver with indecent haste and murmured apologetically, are we saved by the insistent ringing of a telephone? I wonder what excuse people used before it was invented?

Jonathan covered the mouthpiece and smiled at her. 'Kate, you get off, I'll fix things here. Just let Mary know that you're going.' He waved his free hand impatiently. 'Go on, now. There's no point in hanging about.'

Kate moved stiffly from her chair. Tears threatened again. Here was somebody else who didn't want her.

Didn't anybody want her? she asked herself miserably, leaving the room quietly to an encouraging smile from Jonathan. Mechanically she went through to Reception and told Mary Potts that she was going on leave. 'Sick leave, I suppose you'd call it,' she explained. 'Jonathan's adamant about my needing a rest. He will sort things out about duties and so on.'

Mary was sympathetic. She had always felt rather guilty about her attitude towards Kate and Jonathan, never having shown whole-hearted approval of their liaison. Now, however, she saw the onset of a more threatening situation: the dominant Oona Makepiece would surely take Jonathan away a great deal. This was not something which Mary Potts relished, and, despite her peculiar ways, she had a genuine affection for Kate.

'You do need a break, Kate. You've been working so hard for months now, and what with the bombing and everything. Where will you go at this time of year?'

'I don't know yet. It's happened rather quickly. I feel rather as if I've been turfed out into the wilderness.'

'Oh, please don't feel like that.' Impulsively, Mary stretched out a hand and patted Kate's. 'Just go and enjoy yourself and come back like a giant refreshed. We'll all miss you.' Her stern face crumpled into a smile. Kate could have kissed her. She was the first person that morning who seemed genuinely concerned, not just for her present state, but for her return to normal.

She drove home by way of St Ethelreda's, the eleventh-century church which she had attended since she was a small girl. All the gravestones were familiar, old family names, most of their descendants patients of the practice and well-known to her. The Carters, the Spooners. Mary Potts' parents, and the Greens, and Reginald, the late husband of old arthritic Mrs Brown, with whom she had talked that morning.

They were all here, in their neat, or not so neat, graves. Most of them were visited by the surviving members of the family at least on anniversaries, or Christmas or Easter. Leaning, grey, lichen-covered headstones proclaimed many names and dates, but none were so plentiful or well represented as the North family's. Stretching back to almost illegible dates, fifteen hundred and twenty, said one stone, the last entry on a list of four, all enclosed within an iron-railing fence.

Kate found it soothing, walking around the churchyard until she had circled it and arrived back at the front porch. She let herself in through the heavy oaken door, lifting the iron latch as quietly as possible.

There was nobody inside. The altar was filled with late dahlias, roses and, overwhelmingly, chrysanthemums, filling the air with their astringent scent, mingling with traces of incense and candle wax.

She wandered round the church as she had wandered round the graveyard, comforted by the quiet and solitude and age of this place of worship. 'All will be well, and all manner of things will be well,' read an inscription on a brass tablet mounted on the north wall. And the more usual, 'Suffer the little children to come unto me,' carved round the font in beautiful Italianate letters.

Behind the font was the vestry and the winding narrow stairs to the belfry, the most ancient part of the church. Hidden behind the stairs, a door led down to the musty old crypt, usually kept closed and displaying a notice warning of broken steps beyond. To Kate's surprise, the door stood ajar. She couldn't remember the last time it had been open.

Perhaps the rector was down there, or one of the workmen who'd recently been doing repairs to the roof. Or maybe a tramp, or worse, vandals. Curiosity and a faint noise coming from below overrode caution. She pushed the door further open and began descending the slippery, broken steps into the gloom below. There was a small grille let into the top of the wall, concealed from the outside by bushes, but letting in a faint greenish light sufficient to illuminate the crypt.

Something moved from behind the sarcophagus in the middle of the room. Kate let out a muted scream, and then a wobbly sigh of relief as the rector's black and white cat, Dicken, streaked past her and up the steps with a screech of surprise. He had obviously been as frightened as she.

Now that the noise had been accounted for, and her eyes were accustomed to the dimness, Kate found herself trying to read the inscription on the plinth surrounding the stone coffin. The age-old silence that pervaded the crypt calmed and comforted her as nothing else had for weeks. Here among the coffins of those long dead her misery seemed less poignant, more manageable. She felt that perhaps, in the end, she might come to terms with her despair.

The effigy of a knight in the full armour of the twelfth century lay on top of the stone coffin. Visor raised, stern, aristocratic profile exposed, hands crossed on the hilt of a massive sword stretching from chest to feet, the effigy looked the epitome of a noble knight. A dragon-killing knight, a knight capable of rescuing a maiden in distress.

Kate rubbed some grime away from the inscription, and read it.

> Here lyethe the mortal remains of Sir Rowland North, baronet. A noble gentleman, 'Le Parfait Chevalier'.

The script wasn't as plain as that; it was written in a mixture of medieval English, Latin and the rather unusual French phrase. There was a lot more besides, in Latin. She could make out dates and references to the North family, to the land and the manor house. But it was the phrase, 'Le Parfait Chevalier', that made an impact.

Kate leaned heavily against the coffin. The Perfect Knight, she murmured, translating the words. Another Rory from another time. A noble gentleman. Suddenly she knew that this was true of her Rory. He too was a noble gentleman. Standing here in this dim, sacred place, she wondered how she could ever have doubted it.

Her heart lifted. 'All will be well, and all manner of things will be well,' she quoted as she climbed to the top of the steps. Carefully she closed the door behind her, and walked down the aisle to the altar, where she knelt for a few minutes in prayer.

She knew now what she was going to do. She would take a week's holiday, though she still wasn't sure where, and come back and sort out all her problems. She would talk to Jonathan and Oona, and make sure that they didn't feel guilty about loving each other. And then she would talk to Rory. He might be more difficult to convince about her change of heart, and perhaps have reservations about her feelings concerning his past, but she would make him understand that she had never doubted him. That she didn't suspect him of keeping unnecessary secrets.

When she came out of the church, the sun had broken through the overcast sky, a pale, watery imitation of the brilliant summer suns of the last few months, but sunshine nevertheless. She felt like singing.

She sat in her car parked beside the flint wall of the churchyard and gave herself up to daydreaming about a future with Rory. For such was her euphoria that she had no doubt that a future together would be theirs.

She felt like going straight to Rory and telling him of her complete change of heart. She wanted to share her joy with him, at the lifting of the burden which she had been carrying, but she also wanted to hug it to herself for a while.

'Besides,' she muttered out loud, 'he'll think I'm absolutely crackers going back within the hour with such a story.' She giggled softly. It was the first time for weeks that she'd been able to express anything like spontaneous merriment.

She switched on the engine, released the handbrake and prepared to drive off. She looked in her mirror and turned her head to look through the rear window. The old people's home across the lane hove into view as she peered to see that all was clear for her to cross to the left. As she expected, it was. She started to pull out, still glancing occasionally behind her to where the drive to the home opened on to the lane.

The flat lawns and low bushes in front of 'Runnymeade', gave her an uninterrupted view of the old, gabled house. Surely, that was a wisp of smoke coming from a third-floor window? No, it couldn't be. For a long moment Kate gazed at the house, her head turned at an uncomfortable angle, then she put the car into reverse and shot back towards the drive of the rest-home.

As she manoeuvred to go face forward up the drive, a sheet of flame consumed the smoke that had been drifting out of the window.

She jumped out of the car and raced towards the front door, ringing and banging on it as soon as she reached it and found it locked.

A startled young auxiliary nurse opened the door. Kate pushed her aside and made for the stairs. 'A fire!' she gasped. 'Upstairs, sound the alarm.' Why hadn't the alarm gone off automatically? she wondered.

The nurse stared at her. 'Go on,' shouted Kate

halfway up the broad stairs. 'Break the glass and then get everybody out.'

The stairs to the second floor were steeper and narrower. There was a lift, but only the fittest residents lived up there.

Against all the rules the fire door at the head of the stairs was propped open. An elderly man, whom she recognised, appeared as she arrived there panting. 'Brigadier,' she gasped, 'there's a fire. Go downstairs, now, at once.'

The old gentleman stood looking frail and shocked for a moment, then he seemed to pull himself together. 'Better warn Mrs Thompson,' he said gruffly, 'and Miss Lord. And there's a new lady at the end of the passage; I think she's there now.'

'You take the others down, Brig, please. The fire must be in the new patient's room. I'll get her. Close the fire door behind you.'

'Right, Sister, will do.'

At that moment, the fire alarm started ringing, shrilling insistently. Kate ran down the corridor. The bathroom door opposite room five stood open. Kate dashed in and grabbed two towels hanging on a rail and soaked them under the bath tap, then draped one over her head and used the other to shield her hands. She crouched down and pushed open the door to room five.

Smoke and flames belched out over her head. She recoiled, choking and coughing.

She dropped to her knees and crawled across the room towards the bed. The foot of the bed was alight, but the rest of it, though shrouded in smoke, was not on fire. A prone form lay on it.

The door had automatically closed behind her, but the gush of fresh air had fanned the flames, sending them rolling and crackling across the ceiling. The fire was concentrated on the window and other side of the room, but it was gradually creeping up the bed and along the skirting board towards the door.

Kate wondered why the patient was still lying on the bed. Surely she couldn't be asleep, or had the smoke already rendered her unconscious? Whatever the reason, she didn't rally when Kate shook her shoulder or shouted at her to get out.

The flames were beginning to lick around the patient's feet. Kate pulled her off the bed and she landed on the floor with a sickening thud, but still didn't rouse. Throwing the second wet towel over the woman's face and chest, Kate began dragging her towards the door. Her own chest was beginning to ache. Every breath was painful.

With a tremendous effort she dragged open the door, and, holding it back with her shoulder, hauled the patient through into the corridor.

A rush of smoke and flames went with her. As the door started to close behind her there was a crash as something in the room fell into the doorway, wedging it open. The corridor rapidly began to fill with smoke. For a moment she wondered if she should try to clear the obstruction and close the door, but realised that this was beyond her strength.

'Not far now,' she whispered, as much for her own comfort as the patient's. The back of her neck felt terribly hot, she could smell hair burning and realised that it was her own. With a frightened whimper she stopped pulling the old lady for a second and rubbed at the towel over her head. The towel was alight. She threw it away and rubbed with her bare hands at her singed hair. Her hands hurt, but she must have succeeded in putting out the flames for it no longer felt as if her neck was on fire. Still the patient didn't stir.

The raw, acrid smoke hurt her nose and throat, making her cough and wheeze as she tried to breathe. Tears were streaming down her face. The distance to the top of the stairs seemed endless, but at last she got there. The fire door was closed, bottling up the smoke in the corridor.

Somehow she would have to get it open and then drag the old lady down the stairs. Head first, she told herself, so that I can control her fall a little. She wished that she had something to make into a makeshift sling or soft stretcher. Amazingly, she was able to recall with great clarity that the text books instructed rescuers to roll victims in mattresses or bedclothes, but in this case the bedclothes and mattress had been on fire.

Should she have tried to grab something from one of the other rooms in passing? No, the important thing was to get the patient down the stairs. For the first time since speaking to Brigadier Moles, she thought about time and whether anyone would come to help her. She had no idea how long it had been since she'd first run up the stairs, whether it was minutes or hours. It felt like hours. She hurt all over, inside and out.

She was aware of a noise above the awful crackle and hiss of flames moving relentlessly along the corridor. It was some moments before she realised that it was the smoke alarms ringing at the head of the stairs. There were other sounds too. People sounds. Voices and movement. Her chest was hurting so much now that she dared not take another breath. Don't breathe, she told herself, don't breathe and it will stop hurting. She scrabbled at the handle of the fire door. . .

For a moment the air seemed less hot, less smoky. She took in a deep breath, but the pain in her chest was so bad that she wanted to scream. She heard a strange gurgling, rattling sound. Hands were round her body, they hurt, she cried out again. Muffled sounds came and went. A voice, yes, it was a voice, said something close to her head. Her head felt sore. Words came out of the voice, a voice that she knew, but whose voice, whose? 'Rory,' she tried to say, but her tongue wouldn't move properly. It seemed stuck to the roof of her mouth.

The words sounded clearer now. 'Kate? Kate, darling, it's me, Rory.'

She tried to say that that was what she had said, but her sore lips and immovable tongue wouldn't frame the words. She so much wanted to let him know that she could hear him. Some jumbled speech spilled out from her swollen mouth, she felt tears welling up in her eyes and spilling down her hot cheeks. Even the tears hurt.

Rory's voice now sounded very strong, loud, too loud. She moved her head to one side. Rory was saying, 'We're taking you downstairs, Kate. You'll be all right, dear girl. I'm here. I'm here. I've given you something for the pain, love.' His hand, a hand that she would know anywhere, large, but slim and very brown, stroked her cheek and pushed back a few strands of hair.

She was floating down the stairs. She felt entirely, absolutely happy. He was here, it didn't matter what was happening, where she was going, he was here beside her. 'Rory,' she rasped out, and this time she heard herself saying his name. 'Patient, is she——?'

'She's fine, she'll be OK. She had a stroke.'

'Oh, good, that's why she wouldn't move.' Her voice was thick and croaky but Rory seemed to understand.

'Yes, love, that's why. Now go to sleep, please, dearest girl.'

Sleep; she started to drift off. As long as he was here, she could sleep. 'Rory——' She wanted to squeeze his hand but her own hands wouldn't work, they were sore, so sore.

'I'm with you, love. I'll always be with you.'

She sighed a deep sigh. It hurt her chest, but she didn't mind. Just as long as he understood. As long as he knew what had happened to her, not in the fire, but before. . .

She didn't know how long she slept, but when she woke up, fully alert within seconds and recalling all that had happened, she found herself in a hospital bed. Her hands and arms were encased in what she recognised as antiseptic and healing solution plastic bags. A folded plastic oxygen tent stood a little way from the bed. A drip was being fed into her upper arm just above the point where the protective bag finished. Her neck felt stiff, there was a collar with liquid in across her back. She was propped up, half on her side in the high bed.

Sitting in a chair next to the bed, one hand on the pillow close to her face, sat Rory, fast asleep. His long, lean face was almost colourless, except for a fringe of dark stubble round his chin. His blond hair looked ashen-grey. Kate smiled through cracked painful lips. He had stayed with her. Of course he had stayed. He'd promised, and a perfect knight always keeps his promise. She wanted to laugh, but no sound came through her scorched chest and lips.

His eyelids flicked suddenly open, he turned his head, and his sea-green eyes stared straight into hers. 'Kate, darling, you're awake.' He smiled, and his smile seemed to swallow up the tired lines round his mouth. He heaved himself out of the chair, leaned over the bed and kissed her tenderly, not on her sore mouth, but low on her cheek, near her mouth. 'My darling, darling girl,' he murmured.

'You stayed,' mouthed Kate, through swollen lips.

'Of course I stayed, what else would I do, you silly, lovely girl? I love you. Nothing else matters, nothing else is important, except that you get well, and strong, and become your usual happy, composed self.'

'But will I, ever?' Unexpectedly, tears welled up and overflowed, searing down her still inflamed cheeks.

'Of course you will, my love.' One lean brown hand stroked gently through her short, crisp hair, lifting it from the still tender scalp, the other found a tissue and mopped gently at her eyes, drying her tears.

He was so sure, while she was still full of questions in spite of knowing where her heart lay. All those resolutions that she'd made before the fire. She had been going to face him with her new-found certainty. She had been prepared to wait for him to accept her change of heart. Yet now it was he who was sure of himself and his feelings for her, and she who needed to know what had happened to make him change his mind about her.

'Why did you go away from me?' she asked, forcing the words through stiff lips.

'Because I thought that you and Jonathan were in love. That you wanted each other. There were enough problems for you both. Your mother, and Thomas and Uncle Matt. I thought that I was an intrusion. That my presence was making life even more difficult for you, my love. It was the last thing that I wanted, to add to your difficulties.'

'But later, when you knew that Jonathan meant so little to me? I mean, when it must have been clear that I didn't love him deeply, that he was in love with someone else. Why did you suddenly decide to return to your London practice for most of the time?'

Her lips hurt after this long sentence, but her need to know why he had acted the way he had helped her to ignore the fact that they were cracked and bleeding.

'My dearest dear.' Rory sat on the side of the bed and swabbed her tortured lips with a soothing liquid from a tray by the bedside. He gave her a feather-light kiss, and a trace of blood was on his own lips as he sat back and smiled at her. 'I thought that there might still be something between you both, in spite of your appearing to reject him, and his obvious interest in Oona. I made myself think of my career and the need to give it all I've got. I almost convinced myself that I would be better off without the distractions of a wife and family.'

'And what about your career now, isn't it still the most important thing in your life—won't you be better off without dependants?' A sudden fear struck her, and again she had difficulty holding back tears. 'Rory, please don't pretend; don't say that you love me just because you're sorry for me, because of the accident, or on account of Jonathan's loving Oona. I couldn't bear that. I'd infinitely rather not have you than have you on those terms.'

Rory slipped off the side of the bed where he had been sitting and stood looking down at her, the gold flecks in his eyes gleaming, his lovely mobile mouth quirking at the corners.

'What a fierce interrogator you are, my love!' He grinned broadly. 'Almost your nurse-manager self.' The expression in Kate's eyes told him that she wasn't ready for even gentle teasing. He dropped on to his knees beside the bed so that his face was on a level with hers. 'Dear heart,' he said softly. 'I love you utterly. I wanted, want, only your happiness. I felt guilty about persuading you away from Jonathan.'

Kate frowned, but even furrowing her brow was painful, and she winced with the effort. Rory leaned over and brushed the crease between her eyebrows with his lips.

'You find that hard to believe?'

'Yes,' Kate replied in a whisper.

'Darling, you rebuffed me on many occasions, just when I thought that I was getting somewhere, both before and after the Jonathan and Oona saga began. Honestly, I didn't know what you wanted from me.'

'Did I rebuff you?' The salve that he had put on her lips, or perhaps his kiss, made it easier for her to speak. 'I'm sorry.'

'I thought at one time that you had dismissed me as a common thief because of the rumours that had once circulated. And then, of course, there was Jonathan's obsessional hatred for me—mostly, I now realise, in defence of his mother, whom he adored.'

Kate tried to shake her head but the padded collar and her position made this impossible.

As forcefully as she could, she mumbled, 'No, Rory, no, I never thought you a thief. Once I'd met you, I knew that you couldn't possibly be that.' She closed her eyes and tried to ignore the salty tears welling up beneath the lids and spilling over. Rory brushed them away with gentle fingers.

'Don't distress yourself, love,' he murmured, velvet-voiced.

'But you must understand; please, you must.'

'OK, darling, I'm listening.' He smoothed back her tangled mass of spiky hair, and smiled and moistened her lips yet again with the soothing liquid from the plastic pot on the bedside table.

'I did wonder,' said Kate in a soft but firm voice, 'if Jonathan was right when he said that you would come along and upset everything. He thought that you would steal his father's affection and the practice, and Rory, I wondered if that might be true.' She scrabbled for the right words. 'Not because you were who you were, but because you were exactly what old Dr North needed— a support. Not just an adequate doctor, but someone who could give the patients that extra something. Perhaps it's called charisma. I don't know, but you had it, and Jonathan didn't.'

'Oh, Kate, dear love, if only we'd talked earlier. Poor Jonathan, pushed into medicine to compete for adulation from his parents. He didn't stand a chance.

He should have followed his mother into the world of art.'

'Yes, poor Jonathan. I almost hated you for a little while. You seemed to have everything, and he nothing except scorn and second-hand acceptance by his father's patients.'

'Oona will see him all right. She is just what he needs, just as you are what I need.' Rory was still on his knees. He leaned towards her and kissed her neck beneath her ear. Delicately, he kissed her throat, between the tapes that secured the pad to the back of her neck, and smiled at her tenderly. 'These are almost the only parts that I can decently and intimately reach without hurting you,' he said softly, 'but the day will come when I can love you like this all over.' With small fluttering movements he traced the line of her throat down to the modest V of her hospital gown with his lips and tongue. 'You drive me mad,' he whispered.

Kate achieved a smile of sorts from her tortured mouth. 'You must go,' she uttered. 'Get some rest.'

'Well, there are patients to see,' he said. Reluctantly he left, and Kate drifted into sleep.

The next time she woke, after slipping in and out of consciousness over twenty-four hours, the room seemed to be full of people and flowers. Her mother was there, and Dora, and Jonathan and Rory. A freshly shaved Rory, she noticed, who smiled at her over the heads of the others as they crowded into the room.

Her mother's wheelchair was pushed up hard against the bed, and her mother was stroking her cheek as she opened her eyes.

'Darling,' said Mrs Christy, 'we've been so worried about you, but Rory's kept vigil, as it were, and reported back to us.'

Jonathan bent over the bed and kissed her carefully on her forehead. 'I thought you'd rather it was Rory,' he said softly, gently. 'But I would have stayed if I thought that you needed me.'

Kate's eyes filled with tears. She thought that it was probably the most honest and unhesitating statement that she would ever hear from Jonathan.

'We're right for each other,' she whispered huskily. 'Just as you and Oona are right together.'

Jonathan heaved a tremendous sigh.

They all went away after a while, except Rory. He stayed, sitting at her bedside, stroking her cheeks and occasionally kissing them, reading the many cards and letters wishing her well. They talked quietly of their feelings for each other. Of the stupid pride and unwillingness to talk that had kept them apart for weeks and caused them both so much distress.

They agreed that in the future they would always talk things through, never let the sun go down on their wrath, as the old proverb had it.

Kate, though in pain at times and considerable discomfort most of the time, had never been so happy. Rory spent much of each day with her talking, reading, dozing sometimes, his handsome head resting against the chair-back, long legs stretched out, his hands clasped lightly together. Even in sleep, with his fabulous sea-green eyes hidden, he looked elegant, noble, thought Kate, as she recalled 'Le Parfait Chevalier' stretched out on his tomb in the crypt.

She left hospital ten days later. Her hands and arms were healing well, as were her neck and shoulders. They had been quite badly burned, though she hadn't realised it at the time. Her lovely long chestnut hair had been cut off, since a lot of it had burned anyway, but Rory said that he loved her just as much with short hair.

'You look like a pretty urchin,' he said on the day he collected her from hospital. 'A very young, pretty urchin.' He pretended to look anxious. 'Are you sure, my darling, that you don't think I'm too old for you?'

'Are you trying to get out of marrying me?' Kate asked, laughing.

He kissed her as hard as he dared on her still tender mouth. 'Don't ever think that, or say it, my darling, not even as a joke. I just want to spend the rest of my life making love to you. Married love,' he said firmly lest she should have any doubts about his intentions.

Christmas was a time of great joy for the Christy and North families. They spent the festive season together, Christmas day at Bathurst and Boxing Day at the manor house.

It was a celebration of several events, and a time of new beginnings for them all. A farewell party for Jonathan and Oona, who were due to leave for India on the twenty-seventh. An official engagement party for Kate and Rory, and an unofficial one for Dr Matt North and Maddy Christy, who announced that they intended to marry some time in the following year.

Matt North was going to continue working for a few more months while he and Mike Dolland set up a partnership with the practice across the river, Kate was to organise the administration to cater for the larger group of doctors as senior manager, until she left to marry Rory in April.

Rory was taking up his appointment as Professor of the new paediatric oncology unit attached to a university hospital in Hampshire, in January.

Thomas had a whale of a Christmas. Loads of presents, and the enthusiastic help of the male contingent setting up the elaborate railway system—a combined present from Kate and Rory.

As he said to Kate, when she tucked him up on Boxing Night, 'It wasn't only lots of presents that made it the best Christmas ever, but having lots of family to share it with.'

Out of the mouths of babes, she thought, and said tremulously, blinking back a tear, 'Oh, darling, what a lovely boy you are.'

'Oh, that's good. You won't forget that, will you, when you're Mrs Rory?'

'I wouldn't let her,' said Rory's deep voice from over Kate's shoulder. 'You know, Tom, there's a saying when people get married about gaining someone, not losing someone. Well, in this case think of Kate's and my getting married as you gaining an uncle, not losing an aunt.'

'Oh, that's brilliant,' said Thomas, beaming at them both, though his eyes were drooping with tiredness. 'I think I'll go to sleep now, if you don't mind,' he added politely, and immediately did so.

The church of St Ethelreda was full on the day that Kate and Rory were married. Old Dr North, as her future stepfather, gave her away. Mike Dolland escorted Mrs Christy, and Thomas, immaculate in a kilt of the tartan to which the North family were entitled, followed Kate up the aisle, carefully holding her short train.

To almost everyone's astonishment, including Kate's, Jonathan had flown home from India to be Rory's best man. It was the happiest thing that could have happened to Matt North, and, of course, to Kate and Rory.

They emerged from the church and were greeted by glittering April sunshine.

Kate snuggled closer to Rory. 'My Perfect Knight,' she whispered.

'On the contrary, my darling Kate. My Perfect Lady.'

Mills & Boon

— MEDICAL  ROMANCE —

The books for your enjoyment this month are:

ALL FOR LOVE Margaret Baker
HOMETOWN HOSPITAL Lydia Balmain
LOVE CHANGES EVERYTHING Laura MacDonald
A QUESTION OF HONOUR Margaret O'Neill

♥   ♥   ♥   ♥   ♥

Treats in store!

Watch next month for the following absorbing stories:

TENDER MAGIC Jenny Ashe
PROBLEM PAEDIATRICIAN Drusilla Douglas
AFFAIRS OF THE HEART Sarah Franklin
THE KEY TO DR LARSON Judith Hunte

present
Sally Wentworth's 50th Romance
The Golden Greek

Sally Wentworth has been writing for Mills & Boon for nearly 14 years. Her books are sold worldwide and translated into many different languages.

The Golden Greek, her 50th best selling romance will be available in the shops from December 1991, priced at £1.60.

Mills & Boon

Discover the thrill of 4 Exciting Medical Romances – FREE

FREE

BOOKS FOR YOU

In the exciting world of modern
medicine, the emotions of true love
have an added drama. Now you can
experience four of these
unforgettable romantic tales of passion
and heartbreak FREE – and look forward to
a regular supply of Mills & Boon
Medical Romances delivered direct to your door!

❧ ❧ ❧

Turn the page for details of 2 extra
free gifts, and how to apply.

An Irresistible Offer from Mills & Boon

Here's an offer from Mills & Boon to become a regular reader of Medical Romances. To welcome you, we'd like you to have four books, a cuddly teddy and a special MYSTERY GIFT, all absolutely free and without obligation.

Then, every month you could look forward to receiving 4 more **brand new** Medical Romances for £1.60 each, delivered direct to your door, post and packing free. Plus our newsletter featuring author news, competitions, special offers, and lots more.

This invitation comes with no strings attached. You can cancel or suspend your subscription at any time, and still keep your free books and gifts.

Its so easy. Send no money now. Simply fill in the coupon below and post it at once to -

**Mills & Boon Reader Service, FREEPOST,
PO Box 236, Croydon, Surrey CR9 9EL**

NO STAMP REQUIRED

- - - ✂ -

YES! Please rush me my 4 Free Medical Romances and 2 Free Gifts! Please also reserve me a Reader Service Subscription. If I decide to subscribe, I can look forward to receiving 4 brand new Medical Romances every month for just £6.40, delivered direct to my door. Post and packing is free, and there's a free Mills & Boon Newsletter. If I choose not to subscribe I shall write to you within 10 days - I can keep the books and gifts whatever I decide. I can cancel or suspend my subscription at any time. I am over 18.

EP20D

Name (Mr/Mrs/Ms) _____

Address _____

_____

_____ Postcode _____

Signature _____

mps
MAILING
PREFERENCE
SERVICE